The Minstrel Boy

Also by Richard Crawford

Fall When Hit

Richard Crawford

THE MINSTREL BOY

HEINEMANN : LONDON

First published in Great Britain 1994
by William Heinemann Ltd
an imprint of Reed Consumer Books Ltd
Michelin House, 81 Fulham Road, London SW3 6RB
and Auckland, Melbourne, Singapore and Toronto

A CIP catalogue record for this title
is available from the British Library

ISBN 0 434 00152X pb
ISBN 0 434 143278 hb

Phototypeset by Intype, London
Printed and bound in Great Britain
by Mackays of Chatham PLC

'The Minstrel Boy to the war has gone,
In the ranks of death you will find him.
His father's sword he has girded on
And his wild harp slung behind him . . .'

Traditional

For nearly ten years Stevie Rea had ruled his little patch of the Shankill like a minor and absolute king. He held his court in the clubs and the lounge-bars, dispensing judgements, settling arguments with his fists, famous for his size and the speed of his temper. Strangers would nod to him in the street. Men he had never met would come up to shake his hand and buy him drinks. He had been feared and respected, a man to take notice of, until one grey December morning when a no-warning bomb in a menswear shop left him with a twisting, writhing limp and an aching bitterness towards the other side. Not all the other side, he was careful to remind himself as he lay smoking in the darkened bedroom. Not all of them. Just the bastards who had planted that particular bomb in that particular shop.

He always lay awake in bed long after his wife had dropped off to sleep. Usually he smoked. Angie didn't like him smoking in bed, so he waited until her breathing slowed before lighting up, and afterwards he would put the ashtray on the floor and slide it under the bed so that she wouldn't find it in the morning. It had become one of his rituals. Angie knew all about it but she pretended not to for the sake of peace and quiet.

He pulled heavily on the cigarette, watching the tip glow brighter as he drew. There was rain outside and it pattered softly on the window, coming now and again in gusts with the wind. It sounded like a bloody cold night. It was good to lie there in the darkness with his wife beside him and the rain outside and the faint, faint redness from the clock-radio display. He enjoyed the quiet. Some nights he could hear the distant hiss of the sea on the promenade, and for long, still minutes he would lie in the darkness with his head empty, letting the whispering sound of it wash through his mind.

Most nights he couldn't get that emptiness and his mind would lurch back to the bomb, or the pain in his leg if it had been particularly bad that day. There was always some pain, like a low, steady tone in the back of his mind. Once he had heard a woman on the television pulling a long, sobbing note from the cello and he had thought, that's it, that's the pain. But some days there were sharp, biting pains from what was left of his knee and they were strong enough to make him wince, even now, ten years later.

From that jagged starting point he would let his thoughts ramble where they pleased, lying with one hand behind his head and the other holding the cigarette on his chest. Sometimes there would be noise in the street outside; the sound of passing feet, male or female, walking quickly or shuffling, this pavement or the far one. He had become an expert in footsteps. Some of the neighbours he could recognise by the sound of their walk, especially old Maguire two doors down who wore a shoe with a built-up sole. He was a Fenian but he wasn't a bad Fenian. He walked with a hurried, dragging step. Now and again there would be a fight, or the spill-over of a fight from the bar on the main road. Voices raised in anger, the usual cursing and swearing to get the courage up, maybe a woman shrieking in fear or rage. It was good to lie in bed with the curtains drawn and the warmth of his wife beside him and listen to it all going past outside. Mind you, he reflected, there were more drunks around these days, staggering from wall to wall, shouting and yahooing. Young fellows, too. Wouldn't have happened in his day. You got drunk, you fell over, you went home. You didn't wander the streets looking for aggravation.

The town was going downhill, he decided. He had taken the family there eight years before, when the compensation had finally come through. He hadn't been able to face the city any longer. Too much muttered sympathy, and the pain of seeing what he once had been reflected in people's eyes. Younger, faster men had taken over his patch and he had felt like an outsider in his own land, limping slowly through the back doors of the bars and lounges like a ghost, unnoticed.

So he had bought the house outright and they had a fresh start and it had been a good move, good for Angie, good for the boy. They were better off out of the city. The air felt cleaner here, fresher, and there was always the vast grey expanse of the sea open on one side. It always made you feel small and sometimes that was a good thing for a man.

He found his thoughts at a standstill and he pulled on the cigarette, thinking of nothing in particular, until the leg began to ache again. Bastards. He shifted the leg slightly beneath the quilt, trying not to disturb his wife. It would be difficult to sleep with this pain but then maybe that was a good thing. There was a recurring dream which often came back to him, a picture frozen, like a photograph, but with noise and shouting and sirens in the background and that feeling always in his stomach, as if his body was dropping away from him. The same picture, every time; tarmac, debris, shards of glass; his leg stretched out in front of him, bent and twisted like he had four knees and the blood pumping out of the untidy hole in his jeans. That was the first thing he had seen after the bomb and in ten years the image had never left him. Bloody bastards.

He lay until half-past one and still didn't feel tired. He didn't do enough during the day to make himself tired, that was the problem. The bloody doctor was right, clean-living ponce that he was. He was too bloody clean by half, that one. You never could trust men who were too clean. And anyway, all he ever came out with was take more exercise and lay off the fags and I hope you weren't drinking again, Mr Rea. Couldn't do anything for the pain, though. Doctors couldn't cure this pain anyway, he thought, this pain is in there for good, it's in the bone. For ever.

The clock-radio winked its bright red figures at him. Outside the wind had strengthened, spattering the rain against the window like handfuls of gravel. Colin should be home by now, he reflected. He wondered idly where the boy might be. He was usually home by one o'clock on a Friday night. There was no cause for worry because the boy could take care of himself all right, Stevie had seen to that, bad leg and all. Although Angie would worry, if she were awake. But Colin would be all right. There had probably been a function on at the golf club and Colin had volunteered to stay on to help clean up, that would be just like him, always letting people take advantage. He would be all right.

But still he lit another cigarette and lay awake and listened, thinking of nothing in particular but listening carefully to all the distant night sounds of the town. A siren wailed miles away before fading gradually into the background and it pushed a tiny seed of worry into the back of his mind, irritating him. For Christ's sake, he told himself, this isn't the city, this is a small town, nothing ever happens here. Besides, the boy had a bit of sense about him, he knew when to stand and fight and when to make a run for it and he could run like a whippet; he was a good lad and he would be home soon and there was no need to worry.

The clock was winking 3.43 when he heard the familiar clacking footsteps on the pavement and the crunch of the key in the front door. He listened as the door banged closed and the snib clicked on, followed the heavy footsteps up the stairs to the small bedroom and heard the bedroom door closing. There was a tiny, hissing noise of the radio in the other bedroom. What sort of bloody time was this to come in? He needs a good clip round the ear, the same boy, and he's not too old

5

for it, either. He reached out to the ashtray beside the clock and stubbed out the half-smoked cigarette, twisting it roughly to and fro. I'll talk to him in the morning, he decided, leaning out of the bed to push the ashtray under the valance. I'll have a few words with the little git. He shifted his leg again and eased his head gratefully down on to the pillow and eventually drifted off to a troubled sleep.

Colin woke at ten o'clock, still tired. A watery grey daylight was seeping in around the drawn curtains, casting a pale light across the untidy bedroom. He could smell his track shoes by the side of the bed. Jesus, he thought, stretching out a hand and fumbling for his watch. I'll never get used to this.

He lay still for a long time, listening to occasional cars splashing through the puddles in the street outside. He lay on his stomach with his face turned towards the plain woodchip wallpaper. It was warm and cosy under the duvet and the air in the bedroom was cold and there was nothing much to get up for anyway. He could hear his father moving around downstairs, clattering cups and the kettle and then the whoosh of the taps and the click of the switches. He must be in bad form, Colin reflected, not really caring. The worse the mood, the more noise he made banging around the house. Bad tempered old git.

At half-past ten he listened to the local news on the radio and five IRA men had been shot dead by the SAS near Pomeroy and Colin lay on his back and clenched his fist above his head, punching the air. That's the way to do it, he thought, wipe the bastards out. Even the news-reader seemed quite cheerful about it. There weren't many details and he made a mental note to watch the TV news that evening. By then the TV crews would have been there and all the news would have come out. It was good when it was the other side who were killed, that always put you in good form for the day. Five less terrorists. He stared up at the ceiling and went through his fantasy again, the camouflaged jacket fantasy where he was ambushing a gang of terrorists and killing them all in one burst from the hip, letting one of them live because he surrendered in time. In all his fantasies he tried to slip in a bit of chivalry, just to keep himself one level above the IRA. They never gave anyone a chance to surrender.

He lay in bed for an hour and then eventually pulled himself out into the cool air and shrugged quickly into his old, warm Aran pullover and a thin pair of jeans. He felt himself shuddering at the cold. I'm too thin, he thought, too thin and bony. I need more fat on me, to keep me warm. He hurried down the stairs. His father was in the living room, sitting in front of the television with his bad leg stretched out in front of him and the remote control dangling from his hand. The television was on, a mid-morning chat show with taped audience laughter but the old man wasn't watching it, frowning instead at a point on the wall behind.

'Did you see the news?' Colin asked.

'I did.'

'That was a good bit of work, wasn't it?'

'It was.'

There was something annoying the old bastard because he was usually more cheerful when something like that had happened. Sometimes he would even smile, but this morning his face was stiff and clamped looking.

'Something wrong?' Colin asked.

'Where were you last night?'

'I was working late.'

'Your arse. Nobody works that late. I was waiting up half the night for you.'

'Well, you shouldn't have bothered.'

Colin sat down in the kitchen and poured out a bowl of Sugar Puffs, all his good humour gone. Bollocks, he was thinking, bollocks, you lie awake all night anyway, you senile old bastard, I've smelt the cigarette smoke. You'll probably set fire to the house some day and get us all killed.

'You've been late home four times this week,' his father shouted in.

'That's right.'

'You're trying to tell me that the bar was open late four times in seven days?'

'I'm not trying to tell you anything. I was working late. You can believe that or not, whatever you want.'

'I'm not that bloody stupid, son!'

The old bastard is working up to a fight, Colin thought, pushing spoonfuls of Sugar Puffs into his mouth without tasting them. He had that brittle, set look about him, the particular face he always had when he was after some trouble. Probably it used to scare people, when he looked like that, back when he was 'Big Stevie Rea'.

'So where were you?'

Colin said nothing and went on eating, staring down at the table-top.

'Well?' Stevie asked. He had come into the kitchen and was leaning against the door, watching, his mouth slightly open and his cheeks tense. His eyes were glittering with anger. Eventually Colin stopped eating and looked deliberately across at him. He wanted to explode, to pick up the bowl of cereal and throw it at the door, to gather up his clothes and his guitar and disappear into the sunset.

'Look. I was working. I had a hard night. I'm tired. Would you get off my bloody back!' He shouted the last few words, slamming his hand down hard on the table-top. The handle of the spoon clacked loudly on the formica surface and the bowl jumped, splashing a little pool of milk and cereal. They stared at each other for a few moments, eyes locked, tempers seething. Ten years ago he would have slapped the head off me for that, Colin thought. He'd have broken my nose for that.

The kitchen seemed suddenly and heavily silent, only the drip of the tap and the whispering murmur of the television in the next room. Colin felt the anger boiling in his chest. There was nothing to argue about and it was pointless to go on and both of them knew it but the old man felt he hadn't finished it yet and he would be scrabbling for another way in.

'Your mother was worried.'

Bollocks, Colin thought. 'She knew I'd be late,' he said. 'I told her.'

The old man opened his mouth again, then closed it and Colin knew that the argument was over. The tension slipped out of the air like gas from a ruptured balloon. There was nothing to fight about, no reason, except that the old fellow liked to take his pain out on someone else. That, and the fact that he had always been a nasty bastard anyhow. Stevie looked down at the carpet, glanced towards the sink, sniffed. He looked about ten years older. Then, without a word he turned suddenly and hobbled quickly back into the living room. You poor old bastard, Colin thought. You've no one left to fight with, that's your problem.

He could remember when his father had been tall and hard, with thick brown hair brushed back from his forehead and dark hair growing over the tattoos on his forearms. He had 'UVF' across a Union Jack on his right arm and 'Death or Glory' on his left. He kept odd hours in those days, often coming home at night drunk to fall on the settee and sometimes sleep there, curled up like a baby with his big leather coat dragged around himself. Sometimes his knuckles would be scraped and bleeding. In the mornings he would lurch around the house burping and farting. The stale smell of drink on a man's breath always reminded Colin of the morning.

He had spent his childhood in the shadow of his father's name. He had been 'Big Stevie's son'. The school bullies had left him alone, wary of his father, and strangers would stop him in the street to ask him how his da was. Colin had no heart for fighting but his father insisted on teaching him some moves and the reputation did the rest, so he rarely had any kind of trouble. He was nine when the bomb shredded his father's leg.

He remembered a time of hospitals and taxis and the neat front rooms of his relatives' houses, his aunts sniffing and embarrassingly quiet. His mother had cried a lot. Then the visits had settled down into a routine of the hospital after school and his auntie's house at weekends, and in the next six months he watched his father growing old. He watched his shoulders sagging, and his skin drying and wrinkling. With each successive visit he saw the hair becoming lighter, and on the hands which lay limp outside the neat hospital blankets he saw the veins become bluer and more pronounced. Ten years in six months. They put pins in his leg and patched up the flesh but there were still great pale gaps and craters where the muscle was missing, and the leg would never work properly again. It was like a death sentence for the old man. The old Stevie died in the bomb, and what was left was only a wasted, hobbling shadow.

He was six months in hospital and another year in bed and when he managed to limp back onto the street he found his people had forgotten him; he had been away too long from the bars and the clubs, too long out of circulation, and his place had been taken. There had been no contest or struggle, just a gap into which the younger men had moved. And Stevie had stayed at home ever since, hobbling from the television to the kitchen and back to the television, half-afraid of the reputation he had lost.

Colin finished his breakfast and rinsed the bowl under the tap before going back through the living room. The chat show had given way to a consumer report on baby pushchairs but his father was still slumped in the armchair staring past the TV.

'When's Mum due home?' Colin asked. He stood by the door waiting for a reply but none came. Stevie didn't even move his eyes, and after a few moments he raised the remote control slightly and casually changed the channel. Well, fuck you too, Colin thought. He turned and went upstairs and banged the living room door as hard as he could.

It was a sharp November day, with a cold wind slicing in from the sea and the high tide foaming up to the black rocks at the edge of the promenade. The horizon was a flat line between two shades of grey. Colin walked the length of the promenade on the seaward side, with his head down and his hands deep in the pockets of his reefer coat. The weather by the sea never got him down the way it did in the city. No matter how bad it became in the depths of the winter there was always something clean about the rain and the wind, like it was new weather. The weather in Belfast was old, rusty weather which had been around too long and which everyone had cursed.

The wind cleared his head, and he tried to push his anger to the back of his mind. It was just the old bastard's way and you couldn't blame him all that much, not if his leg still hurt the way he claimed it did. He thought his mother was far too good to the old man.

14

She took too much in silence. As far as she let him go, Stevie would always try to push a little further, always trying to get a little more. Now and again he would go too far and she would turn on him with surprising vehemence and he would shrink back a little, frightened, because she was his lifeline and he knew it. She doesn't turn on him half enough, Colin thought.

He walked past the harbour and headed up the hill towards the far end of town. The place was empty, just a few old women in bulky coats and polythene headscarves battling against the wind, dragging along their empty shopping trolleys. In the summer the promenade would be packed with tourists and trippers, bustling along the pavements and jamming the road with their cars, but in the winter the town was cold and empty, the shop fronts blank and sullen and all the doors closed against the wind.

The Anchor Inn was on the Coleraine Road, a squat, grey brick building with mock tudor windows and a big, orange illuminated sign above the doors. It was too ugly a building to appeal to the tourists in the summer and so the clientele were mainly local and they didn't care how it looked.

Hutchy was waiting for him outside the locked double doors, the hood of his German parka pulled up over his big head and his hands stuffed deep into the pockets, shifting on his feet to keep them warm.

'All right, Hutchy?' Colin called.

'I'm bloody well foundered standing here! I wish that old git would hurry up and open the bloody door – '

As he spoke there was a slamming of bolts from behind the big steel plated doors and they suddenly swung inwards. The bald top of Mickey Kerr's head appeared, as he bent down to lock the doors open.

'About time,' Hutchy said.

'What's your hurry?' Mickey retorted easily, turning slowly away and lumbering back into the bar.

'Twat,' Hutchy said under his breath. They pushed through the inner doors and into the empty lounge, into the coarse, dry smell of stale beer and last night's cigarette smoke.

'Where's Picken?' Colin asked.

'He said he'd meet us here. Probably too good to be seen with the likes of us now.'

'He was always a snob, anyhow. Mine's a lager shandy, by the way, Hutchy. Half-pint.'

'Smart, aren't you?'

Hutchy lumbered across to the bar with his shoulders swaying and his head down in that carefully contrived 'hard-man' walk of his. He liked to think he was tough. He was big and red-haired and spotty and had spent the three years since leaving school on the dole, except for a brief spell as a shelf-packer in a supermarket which ended when they caught him trying to steal a bag of sugar. He had no desire to work for a living; if there was something he wanted he would try to steal it, and if he couldn't steal it he did his best to forget about it. As long as his giro cheque arrived every Wednesday and his parents continued to feed him he was satisfied. He hadn't the sense to realise that someday his parents would be gone and he would have to splash suddenly into the real world; he couldn't see much further than the end of his nose.

There had been three of them from second form

onwards; Colin, Hutchy, and a fat boy called Peter Picken, known as 'Piper' after the poem about the pickled peppercorn. Hutchy and Piper had been together since primary school and Colin had been the late-comer but somehow he had fitted easily into the team, discovering a common interest in causing trouble and a mutual disrespect for authority. They had been good times. They bullied the other kids into a kind of hero-worship. The teachers watched them carefully. Hutchy was in trouble most often, not because he was doing any more than the other two, it was just the he was usually the one who was caught. He had no sense of caution or danger. Once they broke into the newsagent's shop across from the school, prising out the frame of a small window in the store at the back and dropping through into the shop. They were loading sweets into their schoolbags when Piper set off the alarm; Colin and Piper bolted but Hutchy was greedy and insisted on staying a little longer, only to discover he couldn't lift himself back out of the window again. The police had discovered him crouched in a corner weeping to himself, but he never said who had been with him.

Hutchy brought back the drinks, spilling them slightly as he set them on the table.

'What about last night in Pomeroy, eh?' he asked happily.

'Pretty good, pretty good.'

'They must have been waiting for them.'

'Oh, aye, they'd have had intelligence.'

'Good bit of work, though.'

'Aye.'

There was a brief blast of cold air as the door opened

and Piper walked in, looking quickly around the empty lounge. For a second or two Colin didn't recognise him; he was leaner, fit-looking, his hair cut neat and short and his skin clear and lightly tanned. He was wearing new Levis and an expensive leather jacket.

'There's the man himself,' Hutchy said.

'How's the boys?' Piper called, grinning. He came over and sat down beside them.

'You've lost a bit of weight,' Colin said. 'Are they feeding you properly?'

'You're just jealous of my new-found good looks.'

'Bollocks. Hutchy, away and get him a drink.'

Hutchy made some remark under his breath and squeezed out from behind the table again, leaving Colin and Piper smiling uncertainly at each other. Colin hadn't expected this amount of strain between the two of them.

'What's it like, then?' he asked at last. Piper shrugged.

'Hard,' he replied vaguely.

'You look fit.'

'It wasn't the fitness, it was the bloody books. Every night, nearly. Working on the books.'

'Oh.'

He wanted to ask more questions but his pride wouldn't allow it, and he knew Piper would be doing enough crowing without anyone having to ask for it. There was a long second of awkward silence.

'I got a job,' Colin said.

'Yeah, Hutchy said. In the golf club.'

'Barman. It's not much, but the money's reasonable.'

His mind made a sudden and unwelcome comparison of the wages of a junior barman and the salary of a young police constable and he felt his face begin to redden.

'Nice place to work,' Piper said.

'Yeah, it is.'

Hutchy came back again and they talked for a while about daft, stupid things and the coolness in the atmosphere gradually disappeared. Although they would never have the same closeness again, Colin realised sadly. All that was finished. Piper had been away for three months and he had changed somehow, matured, as though his growth had somehow been accelerated while the two of them remained trapped in their youth.

'Good result last night,' Colin remarked, 'in Pomeroy.'

'Aye. The SAS don't muck around, do they?'

'Have you heard anything about it? What happened, I mean?'

'No, but I've heard of two of the boys who were killed. Saw the files on them. Bad boys, the pair of them. One of them had killed three UDR men, and the other was involved in a whole lot of other shootings.'

'Well, they're in the right place now.'

'Bloody right.' They sat in silence for a moment, sipping at their beer.

'Well,' Hutchy said after a moment, licking froth from round his lips. 'Did they give you a gun, or what?'

'Aye,' said Piper, cagily. 'Aye, they did.'

'Well, show us it!'

'I can't show it to you here, for God's sake!'

'Why not? The place is empty.'

'That's not the point.'

'Bollocks,' said Hutchy, leaning back in his seat. 'They never gave you a gun at all.'

19

Piper looked as if he was going to retort, then seemed to change his mind. He glanced quickly around the deserted lounge, then leaned over to one side and pulled up his pullover, revealing the rubber grip of a revolver protruding from inside his waistband. Hutchy leaned forward and reached out towards it but Piper twisted sharply away and banged on the top of the outstretched hand.

'Bugger off, Hutchy,' he said. 'That's mine. Keep your hands off.'

'Ah, don't be so fucking touchy.'

There was a strength about him now, an air of command which was new and strange; it was an outward sign of the change which had separated them. Piper was no longer one of the team, he was no longer the youth who had bullied the younger kids and broken into shops for kicks. He had joined the real world.

They had all decided to join the RUC together, sitting in Hutchy's living room after a dull and empty night at a disco with no money and no girls. Hutchy had been the first to suggest it; Colin had never considered it before, but the more he thought about it, the more it seemed the ideal lifestyle. Plenty of money, a bit of excitement, a little power. A real gun. They thought it over for a day or two then one bright spring morning they walked to the local station and filled in the forms together. After that the days had seemed to drag, as Colin waited for the letter inviting him to interview, getting up early each morning to intercept the post before Stevie found it. He hadn't wanted the old man to find out anything about it, not until he was definitely in and almost ready to go. Then he would announce it, sneering at the broken old git. He had visions of himself standing over his father, immaculate in the neat rifle-green uniform with the shiny-peaked cap and the revolver pulling the belt down on one side, straightening his tie before saying goodbye.

He became fascinated by the police. Every time an RUC landrover whirred past he imagined himself sitting in the back with the Heckler and Koch carbine resting across his knees, glaring out of the hooked-open doors, watchful. He leaned the names of all the hardware; Heckler and Koch, Ruger revolvers, Dartex jackets, Hotspur landrovers. Once or twice he followed the uniformed men on their careful beat through the centre of Coleraine, almost imitating their cautious, rhythmic pace.

Then came the interview in Belfast and he had taken the early bus down so that no one would see him in the suit, telling no one. He presented himself at RUC Headquarters in a sudden fit of nerves, acutely conscious of the sweat on the palms of his hands and hoping he would not have to shake hands with anyone. He had never been so nervous in his life, because nothing else had mattered before. And it had gone well, despite the dry mouth and the thumping chest. He had answered all their questions quickly and easily and had only faltered once or twice, he had been confident, he had smiled at the three policemen and they had smiled back. That night his mother was surprised and wary of his unusual cheerfulness. He had come close to telling her that night but had held back, preferring to present a *fait accompli* so there could be no arguments and no way to stop him.

It had seemed such a certainty that the news came

like a blow to the crotch. The letter had been polite, thanking him for his interest but regretfully informing him that his application had been unsuccessful, etc. etc. He had read the letter three times and by the end of it he could hardly see the words through the tears. That afternoon he had walked down to the harbour with Hutchy.

'It's the security clearance,' Hutchy had said. 'Your da's record. They're not going to let you in with that hanging over you.'

'That's got nothing to do with it.'

'Course it has. Wasn't your da in the UVF?'

'He never did anything,' Colin protested, lying to himself.

'Well, that's what it is,' Hutchy said knowingly. 'Bet you any money.'

Later that week Hutchy was turned down, too. Only Piper was accepted. And now here he was, back from his training, a new and polished man. Confident, neat, trim. And different.

'So what about the training,' Colin asked at last, surprised at the hoarseness of his voice. 'Was it as hard as everybody said?'

'Hard enough. Lot of studying. They made us learn a lot of stuff off by heart.'

Us, Colin noticed. Us, meaning me and my policeman friends. Not us, you and me and Hutchy.

'Did you do much shooting?'

'Did a bit, mainly on the Ruger. I'll be doing more of that when I go back for the operational training.'

'Lucky bastard. You going to let us shoot your pistol?'

'What do you think?'

Hutchy shrugged. 'I only asked,' he said easily.

Piper talked for a long while, telling them funny stories about the training, about the instructors and the teachers, the sergeants and the inspectors. He used a lot of jargon and initials which Colin didn't recognise but both he and Hutchy were too proud to ask what they meant. Colin was conscious of a strong urge not to seem too interested; after all, Piper wasn't anything more than he was, he'd done nothing more than Colin could have done, if they'd given him the chance. He sat back in the seat and half-listened and after a while began to try to appear bored. Piper caught it almost immediately, glancing across in mid-sentence. He finished his story then quickly drained his pint.

'Listen, boys, I've got to go,' he said, looking at his watch. 'I've to meet someone in Coleraine in half an hour.'

'Sure you're only here five minutes, for God's sake,' Hutchy protested.

'Nearly an hour, Hutchy, your bloody watch is wrong.' He stood up, adjusted his leather jacket. Colin noticed the bulge over the revolver, now that he knew where to look. 'Well, thanks for the drink,' Piper said, shaking hands with them. It was probably the first time they had ever shaken hands. 'I'll see you again before I go back.'

'Yeah,' Colin agreed. 'Look after yourself. Beat up a few taigs for us, too.' He had thrown the sentence in to see what would happen and he noticed the fast, sharp look and the brief frown. We've lost him, he thought sadly.

Piper had parked his new XR2 outside the bar and

they spent a few minutes admiring it. Hutchy seemed genuinely impressed. Colin felt an odd confusion of jealousy and anger and sadness whirling round in his mind. It was Stevie's fault, he was thinking, it was all his fault. If he hadn't been such a bloody idiot back in Belfast. Wasting everybody's life, not just his own. I should be there too, Colin thought, watching Piper climbing into the shiny new car. I should have the jacket and the car and the gun. It should have been me, too.

At last Piper was revving the car and pulling out onto the main road, his hand thrust up out of the open window, waving farewell as he accelerated up the road towards Coleraine. Colin and Hutchy stood silently for a long time after the car had disappeared, staring up the empty grey road.

'Lucky bastard, eh?' Hutchy said at last.

'Yeah,' Colin replied. 'Lucky bastard. Let's go and get another drink.'

Later that afternoon they walked up to Sefton's house. Sefton was a lay-preacher. He was tall and thin and pale, with his ginger-brown hair brushed neatly in a side shade and a bald spot beginning to show on the back of his head. He wore cheap-looking black rimmed glasses and was always spotlessly, scrupulously clean, as though he had scrubbed himself with detergent.

'I don't know why you hang around with that idiot,' Colin said, as they walked up the avenue towards the house. 'He's as mad as a hatter.'

'He's all right. He's smarter than everyone thinks.'

'I suppose he told you that, did he?'

Colin had known Sefton for nearly two years but

he still found the older man unnerving. Something about the way he held himself or the way he moved around, always in his dark suits and plain black shoes. He would have made a good undertaker.

'I'll tell you what,' Hutchy said knowingly, tapping the side of his nose. 'There's more to him than meets the eye.'

'Oh aye? Like what?'

'Can't tell you that. Need-to-know basis.'

'Bollocks.'

Sefton lived with his mother in a small, pebble-dashed bungalow with two bay windows, on a quiet road well back from the seafront. It was the sort of house people retired to, the sort of house you'd always see the blinds pulled down in. There was a small front garden with a short path and an iron gate that squealed when it moved. He opened the front door to them in carpet slippers with his guitar slung across his chest, and it clunked awkwardly off the wall as he stood back to let them in.

'Hello boys, come on in,' he said, in his resonant preacher's voice, ushering them down the gloomy hallway to the kitchen. 'Sit yourselves down in there. I'll put the kettle on.'

It was an old woman's kitchen, Colin thought, small and old fashioned, the air tinged with a faint smell of gas. There were pale blue and cream wooden cupboards all down one side, some with frosted glass panels in the doors. The floor was covered with neat linoleum. Everything in the kitchen seemed old and worn, but immaculately clean and well-scrubbed. Hutchy and

Colin settled themselves on to hard, straight-backed chairs while Sefton busied himself with the kettle.

'I was just running over a few old tunes there, Colin,' he said over his shoulder. 'Some Johnny Cash. "Ring of Fire", "Folsom Prison Blues". I suppose they're a bit before your time.'

'Just a bit,' Colin agreed. There was a country and western songbook lying open on the small table. Sefton was always on at Colin to teach him how to play the guitar properly, but Colin wasn't interested. The thought of any closer relationship with the man did not appeal to him. He picked up the guitar and began to strum it softly with his thumb. It was slightly out of tune. I'm glad I wasn't here to listen to the singing, he thought.

'Piper's back,' Hutchy announced.

'Is he, now?' Sefton remarked. 'He's finished his training, then?'

'Nearly. Another three weeks to do yet. He's only got the week off.'

Sefton clicked at the lighter and the gas lit with a tiny whoosh. 'I have to admire him,' he said. 'I have to admire anyone who chooses to serve their country at a time like this.'

'He's getting well paid for it,' Hutchy said. 'Brand new XR2 sitting outside the Anchor. Leather jacket. Fucking big gun.'

Sefton winced slightly at the language. 'He'll earn it, Hutchy,' he said. 'He'll earn it. Did you hear about that business in Pomeroy last night?'

'Just what was on the news,' Colin said.

'Five of the enemy killed,' Sefton said, dropping teabags into a teapot. 'Before they could murder innocent people. Those who live by the sword shall die by the sword. The Lord's justice.'

Colin looked away out of the kitchen window. He didn't like the way Sefton insisted on sticking the Bible into everything. There was too much religion about the place. The five terrorists weren't dead because they were of one religion or another, they were dead because they were terrorists. He thought it was generally better to keep God out of things like that, if you had a God. He himself didn't believe in religion. You had your God or you didn't but either way it was your own choice, and nobody else had any right to interfere. Sefton thought he had the right to interfere; that was why he set up his PA system down at the harbour every Sunday and roared and shouted across the promenade about what you should believe in.

'It's nice to see the army hitting back for once, anyway,' Sefton said, pouring out the tea. 'Those men deserve medals for what they did last night. God only knows how many innocent lives they've saved. Sugar, Colin?'

'Yeah. Two spoonfuls.'

'The trouble is, this will turn out to be a flash in the pan. They could do this every other night if they were allowed to, and in a few months there'd be no more IRA scum to worry about. The trouble is, boys, the RUC and the army have had their hands tied behind their backs. They can't work the way they want to, because they're not allowed to. I'll tell you this for nothing; all they'd have to do is hang a few, and the rest of them wouldn't be so bloody quick to pick up a gun. They're cowards at heart. Cowardly murdering scum. I'm sorry I haven't any biscuits, boys.' He settled himself on a small kitchen stool with his cup of tea placed delicately on the table beside him. 'You see, the only thing they understand is force; that's their language. That's how they communicate with us. What the Government has to do is talk back to them in their own language. But of course, no Government that wants re-elected is going to do that. It all comes down to votes and money. It makes me sick.'

'Me too,' Hutchy said.

Colin tuned the guitar and began to pick softly at it, running down a lilting blues scale to end in a twanging bass. Sefton watched in silence as his fingers slipped easily across the fingerboard, envy written all over his face. I don't like you very much, Colin thought. I don't like you very much at all. There was something about Sefton that wound him up like a spring, making him tense and fidgety, so that whenever he left the house the tension would suddenly dissipate leaving him weak with relief.

'You'll have to teach me that one some day, Colin,' Sefton said.

'I'll lend you the book.'

'I've tried the books. I never seem to pick it up right.'

'Just takes a bit of practice, that's all.'

Sefton nodded. They sat around in silence for a while and listened as Colin picked at the guitar. It wasn't a bad instrument, to be honest, too good for the likes of Sefton. It had a good tone. He played the lead break from 'Stairway to Heaven' because he knew Sefton had tried to learn it many times and had never succeeded. Hutchy slurped at his tea. Outside the wind pressed heavily on the window.

28

'Did you speak to your father yet, Colin?' Sefton asked, staring at the guitar. Colin paused, his fingers still.

'No, not yet,' he replied.

'I thought you were going to ask him?'

'I am going to ask him. I just have to pick my time, that's all. He's been in one of his bloody moods for the past week. Nothing pleases him.'

'He could help us a lot, you know. Contacts, information. Advice.'

'He wouldn't be interested. He's been out of all that for ten years. Nobody remembers him.'

'What do you mean, nobody remembers him?' Hutchy protested. 'I was hearing all about him the other day, you know. He was some fellow, in his day.'

Colin shrugged. 'He might have been some fellow, once. Not any more.'

'It wouldn't do any harm, to ask him, would it?' Sefton persisted. 'Just mention it to him casually, in passing. See what he says.' He smiled, revealing a gold filling in the corner of his mouth. 'You never know.'

'All right.' Colin said. 'Alright, I'll ask him. But you already know the answer.'

'Just talk to him, Colin. You can't do more than that.'

They finished their tea and talked for a while, discussing Colin's job and Hutchy's prospects and a supermarket in Coleraine which was planning to open on Sundays. Apparently the supermarket was owned by a Catholic family, which was practically a crime in Sefton's eyes, anyway, and he launched into one of his long and boring speeches about the idolatry of the Church of Rome. His mind was rigid and fundamentalist; he saw things in black and white, right and wrong, he lived by the Bible. Catholics, as far as he was concerned, were heathens who had chosen not to follow the teachings of the Scriptures and were therefore guilty of a heinous crime against God. They deserved punishment, not forgiveness. Colin noticed that Hutchy was stifling his boredom and pretending to be interested. Colin was more open about it, yawning hugely and staring at the kitchen window until at last Sefton took the hint.

'Well,' he said, 'I'm sure you've both heard all this before.'

'Just a few times,' Colin replied. Suddenly he wanted to get out of the house, anywhere away from Sefton and his bloody religion. 'Look, I've got to head on. I have to get ready for work.' It was a blatant lie but it did the job. Sefton saw them to the door, patting Colin gently on the shoulder as he left.

'Thanks for calling, boys,' he called from the front door. 'I'll see you later in the week.'

Outside the air was sharp and cold but it felt almost unbearably clean after the soft warmth of Sefton's house.

'Is he on this planet, or what?' Colin remarked as they walked back down through the town. Hutchy glanced at him briefly.

'Might surprise you someday, the same man,' he said archly.

'You don't really believe all that crap about starting an organisation, do you? Guns? You know him better than I do, Hutchy, but if you ask me all he's interested in is getting his hand on somebody's knee. And if we're not careful it'll be yours or mine.'

'There's more to him than meets the eye,' Hutchy said.

'He told me the other day he's expecting good news soon. I think he means guns.'

'He's probably talking about the Second Coming. Honestly, Hutchy, he's as mad as a hatter!'

'Well, there's a lot of truth in what he says.'

'Like what, for instance?'

'He's right about the Fenians. You can't trust any of them.'

Colin stopped in the middle of the pavement and laughed out loud. 'Don't be such a dickhead, Hutchy,' he said. 'Next thing he'll be telling you the only good Fenian is a dead Fenian!'

He grinned across at his friend but Hutchy's face was bleak and empty and his eyes were humourless. 'What's so funny about that?' he said at last. He turned suddenly and lumbered on down the road and Colin felt a sudden coldness blow through his heart, like winter wind on warm and living skin.

Barry Kelly's room was on the first floor of the clubhouse and it looked out over the lake at the ninth hole. As the new manager the room was one of the perks, and it was provided free of charge. It was part of a larger bedroom which had been partitioned; the elaborate plaster covings lined three walls and stopped abruptly at the fourth, and an ornate ceiling rose was now close to the back wall. Barry didn't care for the room much; the previous manager hadn't lived there, and a series of occasional visitors had given it a scruffy, abused atmosphere. But the window faced east and in the mornings the early sunlight came straight in and flooded the room, and he could lie in bed feeling warm and comfortable, forgetting for a while the cheap white bedroom furniture and the near-threadbare carpet. The original bedroom had two windows and it must have been glorious on summer mornings; it would have been a girl's room, he imagined. She would have been the daughter of the house, and in his mind she was slim and beautiful, with long dark hair and wistful eyes. She would have spent long hours sitting at the window waiting for her lover, looking sadly out across the neatly kept grounds, neat and prim in her long rustling clothes.

Of course there had never been a sad, long-haired beauty. The house had been built by the Villiers family on the site of a previous building dating from the plantation which was destroyed by fire in 1847, the dark stone quarried specially in Moneymore. The Villiers children were all boys. The family fortune had been made in shipping, but the onset of steam and an unfortunate lack of foresight led to bankruptcy and ruin in the last years of the nineteenth century. The house had been purchased by the golf club in 1905, which had probably spared it the attentions of the IRA in the 1920s, and in 1954 it had been extended on one side to form a new members' lounge and dining room. It was a typically Victorian building, squat and grey with steep pitched roofs and arched gothic windows; the untidy complex of outhouses and yards had been converted into locker rooms and store rooms and a large professional's shop.

In the late Fifties and early Sixties the club had been the focal point for the social whirl of the north coast, and it was during this time that the reputation for class and high-living had been earned. Most of the massive silver trophies in the display cabinet in the hallway dated from that period, as did the black and white framed photographs of club dignitaries shaking hands with members of the Stormont government. Since then the clubhouse had changed little. Barry had been surprised at how shabby it had appeared, but he was coming to understand that the run-down shabbiness was all part of the image; we can afford to change, it implied, but we prefer not to.

The first thing he had discovered was that a golf club never closed or stopped; it merely paused for a short while in the middle of the night, like an old woman taking a nap. It was never long after the last of the inebriated die-hards were helped from the bar in the early hours of the morning until the first players were clacking across the yard in their studs with their trolleys trundling behind them, calling and laughing in the still air. That was always the best time of the day, when the mist still hung around the trees and there was condensation on the windows and the wheels of the trolleys left dark green tracks through the dewy grass.

Barry woke late and lay in bed for a while, listening to the distant hum of the hoovers as the cleaners worked in the hallway. He made a mental note to spend a little time with the cleaning ladies; he had been in the business long enough to realise the importance of a good team of cleaners, and it wouldn't do any harm to get to know them a little better. Besides, if you ever wanted to know the bottom line about anything, ask the cleaner.

Eventually he pulled himself out of bed and flicked on the kettle on the dressing table and wandered over to the window: there was condensation on the glass and a small pool of water on the sill. Outside, the golf course stretched off into the distance, before halting at the line of grey, leafless trees which marked the main road. It was a drab winter landscape of dull greens and greys, and even the sunlight seemed pale and watery. It was a still watercolour landscape, except for a pair of small figures in pale blue waterproofs striding purposefully across the tenth fairway. He watched them idly until the kettle switched itself off with a loud click. How can they go out to play golf on a day like that, he wondered?

He made himself a cup of coffee and washed and shaved, squinting at his reflection in the mirror. His hair was receding too fast, and his gut was beginning to show more than it should, and there was a looseness around his jowls which hadn't been there ten years before. Look at you, he thought. Forty-three years old, single, no kids, no ties. You're a real success, aren't you? It was important to always think positively but sometimes it was difficult and he slopped into self-pity, especially in the morning when he looked at himself in the mirror for the first time in the day. His tired, worn body seemed to accuse him; you could have done better for me, it said. It was worst when he considered the next ten years, tried to imagine where he would be when he was fifty-three. He wasn't afraid of loneliness but it was the sadness of the thing which bothered him. He didn't want to have a sad old age. There would be no kids, not now; but then he had become resigned to that, and the thought no longer frightened him. There might be another wife, it still wasn't too late. There was still time. He wasn't too bad-looking for his age, if you discounted the fleshy wobble to the stomach and the sagging, hairy breasts and the fallen arches. He had never thought of himself as handsome but he was clean and tidy and as good a man as you'd get, with only the normal sins and vices. He rubbed at his chin and thought again about growing a beard, and then he thought, to hell with it: I am what I am.

He dressed carefully in his Farah slacks and tweed sports jacket before heading downstairs to work. It was an odd sensation, living in your workplace, and he wasn't yet sure whether it was pleasant or unpleasant. It was certainly easier than standing in the rain waiting for the bus.

At eleven o'clock he opened the main bar himself, sliding up the shutters and testing each of the draught pumps in turn. It was good to stand in the bar on your own, knowing that you and you alone were responsible for everything in there, from the most exclusive bottle of brandy to the last box of matches. And it was a rich bar, too, with exotic liqueurs and extravagant whiskeys and long, thick cigars which cost two pounds apiece. All the shelves were heavy mahogany and the counter was solid oak, polished and repolished until the grain was barely visible. The glasses and bottles shone against the dark wood. At night the bar seemed to glitter like an opened treasure chest and the members would stand around it smoking and drinking, like moths drawn to an irresistable flame.

In daylight it lost some of the magic; the dust showed and the counter was scuffed, although it managed to retain its aged dignity. The sunlight came straight in through the big picture windows facing the bar and shafted down through the lounge, glinting on the heavy crystal ashtrays on the low tables, catching the occasional swirl of dust in the rays. Barry stood behind the bar like a determined soldier behind his barricade of sandbags, reassured by the strength and solidity of his defences.

'Good morning, Barry.' He had come in quietly through the side door and caught Barry unawares, dreaming.

'Ah. Mr Mullan. You gave me a fright, there.'

'Sorry. The wife is always telling me off for it. I'll give her a heart attack one of these days. How are you?'

'The very best. Lager and lime, isn't it?'

'You've caught me on already, have you?'

'I do my best.'

'I'm a creature of habit, God help me. Yes, indeed, lager and lime, thank you.' Mullan took a cigar from his inside pocket and began to unwrap the cellophane while Barry busied himself with the drink. He was the sort of fellow you would trust easily, Barry thought, watching him from the corner of his eye. He looked hard and tough and threatening, with his big frame and his battered face, but all he had to do was turn the pale grey eyes on you and say his first sentence and suddenly you relaxed, you weren't worried any more. He made people feel secure. Barry had already noticed how people relaxed when Mullan was around, as if they thought, it's all right, Mullan's here. Nothing will happen now. He topped up the half-pint glass with lime and set it carefully on top of the counter. 'No staff in this morning, Barry?' he asked.

'To tell you the truth, Mr Mullan, I like to open up myself. It's never that busy this time on a weekday, and it's very pleasant here with the sun and the view out across the course there.'

'It's pleasant all right. It's a beautiful morning out there. How are you settling in?'

Barry shrugged. 'No problems, really. I'm still getting the feel of the place. I don't like to rush into these things.'

Mullan flicked at his lighter and lit the cigar, frowning down at the end of it until the thing was lit. He puffed clouds of smoke from the sides of his mouth, his eyes bright and steady with a hint of amusement. They were quick eyes. Barry felt he was being sized up by an expert. You're nobody's bloody fool, are you, Mr Mullan, he thought.

'I heard about the trouble with Montgomery and Thompson,' Mullan said quietly, watching to see his reaction.

'Did you.'

The big man smiled quickly, pulling the cigar from his mouth and looking around on the counter top. Barry set an ashtray beside him, and was oddly gratified by the quick nod of thanks.

'Bad news travels fast in a place like this,' Mullan said. 'I imagine you weren't too pleased.'

'I hadn't expected it, to tell you the truth. Not here. I've come across plenty of it in my time, mind you. But I think I expected better of a place like this.'

'The Committee meeting is Thursday, isn't it?'

'That's right. They're going to take a vote on it. Whether I stay or whether I go.' Barry was unable to hide the tinge of bitterness from his voice.

'You'll be all right,' Mullan said. He blew a long plume of smoke into the air. 'Those two boys are out on their own. Most of the members of this club are decent people. You'll find the Committee are behind you in this.' He had been leaning forward across the bar slightly, and

38

now he leaned back and drew on his cigar again. 'Mind you, only so long as you keep up the good work.'

The big man smiled at him and he seemed like the most solid thing on earth, more immovable even than the old oak bar, and for the first time Barry began to feel as though he was in with a chance, after all. He was no longer alone.

'Thanks,' he said, awkwardly.

'Not at all. You're a good man, you deserve a decent break. And I'm not going to let those two bigoted bastards drag this club into the gutter, no matter what. Now, are you going to buzz for a waitress or am I going to starve to death?'

He had intended to hand over to the bar staff at two o'clock and spend the afternoon in the office working on the accounts, but by half-past two only Ernie James and the new lad Colin Rea had arrived for work and there was a biggish crowd in the main bar so he felt obliged to lend a hand. Ernie James was almost a fixture in the bar he'd been there so long, but young Rea had started work only three weeks before and he wasn't completely competent yet; still, the three of them worked well together and without awkwardness, managing to avoid bumps and collisions as they reached and stepped and swerved in the narrow space behind the counter. It was pleasant to work behind a bar again with a crowd at the counter and good men working with you. You tended to lose sight of it after a while in the management game, and it was good to sharpen up the old skills again.

The rush lasted most of the afternoon. Ernie kept the

young lad right with the cocktails and liqueurs while helping Barry keep the crowd supplied with pints of lager. The air was full of the sound of conversation and quick bursts of laughter, the smell of the drink and the swirl of the cigar smoke, the loud clinking of the empty mixers into the bottle bin, the quiet hiss and gurgle of the optics and the jingling slam of the drawer in the till. Music to my ears, Barry thought, music to my ears.

The pace slackened off a little around five o'clock and Colin did the rounds of the tables and they washed the glasses as he brought them in. Gradually the hubbub of conversation eased and the groups of customers grew smaller, until eventually there were only seven people left in the lounge and they could relax at last. The three of them leaned back against the worktop and gazed out proudly on the bar, like soldiers who had just survived a vicious combat.

'They've stopped drinking now,' Ernie said confidently. 'Not be long before they're all out.'

'That was an odd rush, for a weekday,' Barry remarked.

'You can never tell in this place, boss,' Ernie said. He was a strange character, Barry thought; small and wiry and nasty looking, but always polite and keen to help. A useful man to have around. Barry tossed his cloth onto the worktop and glanced at his watch.

'I'll be in the office, lads, if you want me,' he said. There was a dull pain in his neck and he rubbed at it as he walked down to the end of the bar then there was a sharp and sudden tug at his other forearm and it was Ernie, standing close and holding him by the arm. Barry felt a quick surge of fear which set his nerves tingling.

'Jesus Christ, Ernie, don't do that to me,' he said. There was a moment of jarring awkwardness. Ernie looked quickly around the bar.

'Look, boss, this thing with the Committee,' he began uncomfortably. 'We just wanted to ... well, we just wanted to say ... we're behind you, you know? If it's any help.'

Barry nodded once or twice, unsure of what to say. He looked down at the barman's hand, still grasping his forearm, and saw the blue tattooed letters 'UVF' on the skin above the wrist. 'Thanks, Ernie,' he said thickly.

Ernie looked down, released his grip, shifted his gaze in embarrassment. 'I'm no saint, boss,' he said. 'I've never claimed to be, either. I've done my share of bad things and someday I'll have to answer for them and that's fair enough. I've just got to live with that. But what they're trying to do to you is wrong. Everybody here thinks so, not just me. We ... just wanted you to know.'

Barry felt his eyes begin to sting and he looked away for a second. 'Thanks, Ernie,' he said at last, his voice breaking. 'Thank you very much. That will be a great help to me. Thank you.' Then he turned quickly and slipped away out of the bar.

Ernie walked back down the bar a little and picked up a pint glass and began to polish it furiously. Ernie was small and slim but he was a tight wee man and there was a vicious streak in him, too. One New Year's Eve in Coleraine he had smashed a beerglass in some fellow's face for next to nothing and he would have been jailed if the golf club hadn't pulled strings for him.

41

Or so everyone said. Colin knew that stories could be exaggerated and he took most things with a pinch of salt but he was still wary of him, nonetheless. He walked casually up beside the older man.

'What was all that about?' he asked.

'What was what?'

'All that head to head stuff, you and the boss.'

'Nothing.'

'Come on, Ernie, I didn't pop out of the river in a bubble.'

Ernie flashed his head round and his eyes were wild and for a nauseating second of fear Colin thought he had miscalculated, then the other man looked down at the beerglass in his hand and gently set it down on the worktop. Colin felt his knees go weak with relief.

'Well,' Ernie said quietly. 'I'm not a man for gossip but you might as well hear it from me as from someone who doesn't know the whole story. Now look, anything I tell you is between you and me and these four walls, is that clear?'

'Yes. No problem.'

'Good. 'Cause if I hear you've been shouting your mouth off I'll beat the crap out of you. Fair enough?'

'All right,' Colin said hurriedly, not sure if he really wanted him to continue.

'Okay.' Ernie cleared his throat loudly, then nodded and smiled at a group of people who were leaving the lounge. 'You can clear that table when I've finished,' he said. 'The boss, Mr Kelly, is the first Roman Catholic manager in this club. In fact, he's the first Roman Catholic to be employed anywhere in this club. Now, I don't know or care what you think about that, as long as you keep your feelings to yourself. The point is, several of the members weren't happy that he was getting the job, and two of them have gone to a lot of trouble to dig up the dirt on him.'

'What sort of dirt?'

'Ah, just a lot of hearsay. Kelly used to run a bar in the Bogside and there were a couple of shootings in it, but then you tell me a bar in Derry where there hasn't been trouble. And his brother was interned in the Seventies. There's a few other stories as well, but what they're basically trying to make out is that Kelly is involved with the IRA in some way.'

'Was he?'

'I wouldn't think so. He's a good man. I know the type that gets involved, and he's not it. But if these fellows convince the Committee that with all the policeman and soldiers who are members here, your man's too dangerous to have around, then out he goes.'

'God,' Colin said. 'That would be a pity.'

'You're right it would. He's the best manager this place has had in years. Do you think any other manager would have bothered his backside helping out in the bar on a busy day? Not a bit of it. Your man's straight with you. He took me into the office on his first day and he says, Ernie, if you've any problems with anything I do or say, this door is always open and for God's sake come and tell me about it. Now that's a good manager. And it's a damn sight more than that old bastard Neville ever did.'

Neville was the previous manager and had been universally hated by all the staff, but he had been a Protestant and he had fitted in and in some people's eyes that was the most important thing. Kelly did seem to be a decent sort of a bloke, though, Colin thought. He seemed to listen when you were talking, and you got the feeling that he would look out for you, if he could. Not bad for a taig. That was an ugly word, 'taig'. He wondered idly where it came from. Don't be vague, kill a taig, went the slogan. It was a poisonous word and it jagged when you said it. Kelly was the first Catholic he had ever really known, but you could definitely tell the difference. There was something about the way they spoke, not the accent but more the rhythm of the voice, and something about the face and the hair, something you couldn't put your finger on but which said, 'not Protestant'. Still, he reflected, if Ernie James liked him then he must be all right. And anyway, they couldn't be all bad.

The lounge was empty by six o'clock and they drew the thick velvet curtains and Ernie went off to the kitchen to get something to eat, leaving Colin alone in the bar. It was that empty, dead time in the evening when the lounge became silent and the silence rang with echoes of the afternoon, the way the tone from a tuning fork lingers on into nothingness. There was nothing to do but empty the ashtrays and restock for the after-dinner rush, and Colin was down on his knees behind the counter when Mullan came in. The big man cleared his throat suddenly and Colin leapt up, alarmed.

'Hello, Colin,' Mullan laughed. 'Sorry if I scared you.'

'Never worry, Mr Mullan,' Colin gasped. 'It's good for the circulation.' He looked down at the beer bottle in his hand. 'The first ever bottle of Skol with finger marks in it.'

Mullan laughed again. 'What about the job, how are you getting on?'

'Oh, pretty good. Everybody's been very good to me. It's hard work, like, but the crack is good.'

'I've been hearing lots of good things about you from Mr Kelly; he's very impressed.'

'Aye, well, he's pretty good, too,' Colin said, embarrassed.

Mullan smiled and hesitated, as if there was something else he wanted to say. Colin waited respectfully, bottle in hand. Mullan was the sort of person you waited respectfully for.

'I was talking to young Picken in Coleraine yesterday,' he said at last. 'He said he'd just passed out of the depot.'

'Aye,' Colin said. 'I was talking to him on Saturday.'

'It's a pity they didn't take you.'

Colin shrugged. 'That's the way it goes, Mr Mullan. Some you win . . .'

'Well, it wasn't for the want of a good reference, I hope you know that.'

'Aye,' said Colin, embarrassed. 'I think it might have been my da's background.'

'Might have been, right enough. Still, no use looking back, is there? You've got to keep moving forward. You can't change the past, but you can change the future.'

They stood in silence for a moment and Colin felt out of place and awkward. 'Can I get you a drink, or something, Mr Mullan?' he asked.

45

'No thanks,' Mullan said. 'I just called in to see how you were getting on.'

'Ah . . . thanks again for getting me the job.'

Mullan laughed shortly. He pulled himself away from the bar. 'I only put your name forward,' he said. 'You got yourself the job.'

Colin nodded and looked down at the floor and put the bottle of beer on to the shelf at last but Mullan still hadn't gone, standing slightly apart from the counter, like a ship waiting to dock. The silence hung expectantly between them. He was a good man, Colin thought, the only policeman he had ever known. He was always ready to pass a word or two with you, not like the younger cops who only moved you on or tried to hassle you. Everybody liked him. He had got Colin the job; he was the sort of person who could pull strings and make people jerk.

'You've been hanging round with this fellow Sefton quite a lot recently, Colin,' he said at last. It was a statement rather than question and Colin shrugged, a little tingle of alarm buzzing at the nape of his neck.

'He's a friend of a friend, sort of thing.'

'You ever go around to his house?'

'Now and again.'

Mullan nodded slowly. He was gazing at Colin with that special look that policemen seem to develop, a look that manages to unnerve without being threatening, which says, I know all about you, boy, so be careful what you say. Colin shifted his weight from one foot to the other and then realised that he was showing his discomfort and felt his face redden.

'I don't want to interfere too much in your life, Colin,'

46

Mullan said. 'You're a good young lad and you've got a future ahead of you. But I'll give you some advice, and if you're wise you'll take it. Steer clear of Sefton. He has no future. Someday soon he's going to fall, and when he does, make sure you don't get dragged down with him. Do you understand what I'm saying?'

'I think so.'

'Good.' Mullan sniffed, then the detective was gone and the middle-aged Rotarian was back, scratching thoughtfully at the lobe of his ear. 'I'll see you around, then. Take care.'

Tuesday morning was grey and wet and miserable and the rain spattered on the bedroom window like handfuls of thrown gravel. Colin lay in bed for a while and listened to the radio, willing himself to get out of bed. The news came on and there had been a shooting in Belfast, some Protestant bricklayer shot dead in his car but the police weren't yet releasing his name. That would be in retaliation for the SAS shootings. Bad news for some family, Colin thought. Some poor woman being told that it was her husband. Sad. It was that kind of day, too, a sad, grieving sort of day.

Stevie was in the kitchen making more noise than usual, fussing about with the toaster.

'Your mother's not well,' he announced.

'What's wrong with her?'

'I'm not a fucking doctor, am I?'

Bastard, Colin thought. He made a mug of Lemsip and took it up to her; he was shocked at how exhausted she looked, sitting up in bed with her pink nightie on and her face pale and doughy without the make-up. She was working too hard, and the strain was showing in the red rims to her eyes and the way the corners of her mouth seemed always tired. He handed her the mug and sat down carefully on the end of the bed.

'How do you feel, Mum?' he asked.

'Rotten. How do I look?'

'Worse,' he smiled.

'Thanks.'

She had been quite a girl in her day. There were old photographs of her in an album in the sideboard, taken in the Sixties, all bouffant hair and thick black eyeliner, stylish-looking. She had been slim and pretty then, always laughing with her hand over her mouth. Now the strain of the past ten years was beginning to show in her skin, her hair, her eyes; perhaps he was only noticing for the first time but she seemed suddenly very small and fragile, the way old women are.

'It's about time you gave up the Saturday job, Mum,' he said.

'Not a bit of it,' she replied, sipping quietly at the Lemsip.

'Seriously, though. Now that I'm bringing in a wee bit of cash.'

'That's your money, love. You earned it, you keep it.'

'For God's sake. It's bound to cost more than twenty pounds a week to keep me in house and home.'

'Well, when you get your first promotion I'll take a wee bit more off you. All right?'

'What about getting that old bastard downstairs to go out and do some work, instead of sitting on his backside all day in front of the telly? He could get a job some-where, even a few days a week. You should kick him out until he brings in his share!'

Angie smiled shakily. 'You should go easier on him, Colin. He's not the man he was.'

'So you keep saying.'

She drained the Lemsip and set the mug on the bed-side table. 'Thanks, love,' she said. 'That was lovely.' She reached out for her cigarettes and lighter.

'And you shouldn't be smoking,' Colin said.

'It's only a wee dose of the flu, that's all. I'm not on my deathbed yet.'

'They're bad for you, that's all.'

'You're a long time dead.' She pulled heavily on the cigarette, closing her eyes as she did so. 'I don't know why the pair of you worry about me so much,' she murmured. 'Every time I get a cold you'd think I was on my last legs, the way you carry on.'

'We're just concerned, that's all.'

She sighed, letting smoke curl out of her nostrils. 'You worry too much.' She smoked for a while in silence, staring up at the ceiling. It was nice to talk to her like this, Colin thought. He hardly saw her since he started work; she was away before he got up in the morning, and he didn't get home until the early hours. It was good to get a chance to talk again. He could never talk to Stevie. Stevie was like a bumper car in the amuse-ments, you tried to avoid him as much as you could but when you did collide you just bounced straight off.

'Your father was so proud of you when you were born, you know,' she said wistfully. 'Told everybody. He went from door to door round the whole street, knocking everyone up and giving everyone a cigar, whether they smoked or not. Took you down to the bar to show you off. That was your first time in a bar, by the way, when you were three weeks old.'

'Talk about under age.'

'He thought you were going to do great things, Colin. He wanted you to be better than he was.'

It was the same old lecture he had heard a hundred times before, when he brought home his school reports and his mother would hide them from Stevie. In his memory she always seemed to have been peeling potatoes in the back kitchen when he came home, and she would quickly dry her hands and examine the report, her eyes flickering down the grades, always hoping and always disappointed. She was convinced that he had some sort of hidden talent which would someday rocket him to fame and fortune, and he was too considerate to enlighten her. He was plain old Mr Average, not good at anything in particular, but capable at most things, if he put his mind to it. He had come to terms with that years ago, but it would probably take her longer. If she ever did. It must be disappointing to be a mother, he reflected.

'I applied for a job a few months ago,' he said. 'I didn't get it.'

'Oh?' she said. 'What was that?'

'The RUC.'

She nodded slowly, and it seemed to Colin that a shadow had fallen across her face. She drew again on the cigarette, very seriously. When she wasn't pulling on it she held it up beside her ear, clasped between two stiff fingers, flicking at the nails of her other two fingers with her thumb.

'I knew about that,' she said at last.

'How did you know?' he asked, surprised.

'Mullan came down to the supermarket one day. He said he gave you a reference.'

'Why did he tell you?'

'I don't know. I think he didn't want to tell Stevie. I don't know why he told me. Wasn't any of my business.'

'You're right it wasn't!' Colin exclaimed. 'I didn't want anyone to know, until I found out one way or the other! He had no right to tell you!'

She was staring down at the rumpled quilt and she looked old and beaten and somehow heavy, as though the weight of years of life was hanging on her, dragging her down. He had never seen her look so old.

'You didn't know, did you?' he asked gently. 'You didn't know I'd been turned down?'

She shook her head a little. All this time and she had still been hoping. Dear God. Colin felt a sudden, hot rush of emotion flooding into his throat; he wished he could hug her, protect her from the reality, become the man she wanted him to be. He felt tears of pity welling in his eyes.

The door opened quickly and Stevie came in with tea and toast, neatly set out on a circular tray. He limped over to the bedside and set it down on the table, lifting the empty Lemsip cup and pushing aside the clock-radio. The toast was blackened and untidily smeared with marmalade.

'How do you feel?' he asked.

'All right. Did you phone the supermarket for me?'

52

'Aye, I did. I said you'd be in when you were better.'

'Who did you speak to?'

'That wee Fenian bastard of a manager.'

'Damien? Oh, he's a nice lad, so he is.'

'He's a bloody wee Pape. Anyway, you keep warm. Keep the heat in.' He turned to Colin. 'And don't you be disturbing your mother.' Colin glared at him in silence. 'Right. If you need anything else, give me a shout.'

He turned and hobbled out of the room, pulling the door to behind him, and they listened as he clumped awkwardly down the stairs.

'That's why I didn't get in,' Colin said, staring at the door.

'What do you mean?'

'The security clearance. That was what stopped me.'

The room seemed suddenly chilly, or perhaps he had just noticed it. The air smelled of nicotine. He watched as Angie pulled the tray onto her lap and poured the tea without enthusiasm. 'What the hell gives Mullan the right to interfere in our lives, anyway?' he snapped, getting up and walking over to the window. Through the net curtain he could see the plain grey facades of the other houses across the street, each one identical except for the colours of the doors. The puddles on the footpath reflected the even grey sky. Everything seemed dull and grey and wet and silent, and suddenly he had a vision of the future laid out before him, day after day, week after week, drifting on towards senility and every day the same. He would work in the bar until he was old, he would live in a grey house like this one, he would perhaps get married and have children who would grow up and leave him and sometime in the future there would be another dull Tuesday morning just like this one and he would be alone, with the even grey sky reflected on the puddles. And none of it would have mattered.

There was a clatter of metal downstairs as Stevie dropped something on the floor. Useless bastard, Colin thought angrily, can't even make a bit of breakfast without breaking something. He turned to face his mother again. She was picking at the charred toast with a knife, shifting it in tiny movements around the plate.

'Don't eat that stuff, Mum, if you don't feel like it,' he said at last.

'Your father's a good man, Colin, believe it or not,' she said, staring down at the tray. 'He has a good heart.' She picked around the toast for a moment, then wearily set the knife down on the tray. 'Take this away, would you, love? I just haven't got the stomach for it.'

'Sure.' He lifted the tray and she slid awkwardly down in the bed, pulling the duvet up around her. She looked old and crumpled as the sheets. 'I'll leave you alone for a bit, then,' he said gently.

'Yes, love,' she muttered, her eyes already closed. 'Thanks.'

He argued with Stevie at lunchtime over something unimportant and left the house with his meal half-finished, his stomach still empty. He walked quickly out of the estate and towards the town, towards the sea, smelling the edge of salt in the fresh breeze. There was enough rain to make occasional ripples in the puddles as he passed them.

Mullan had no right telling his mother about the

application, no right at all. He had big ideas about himself, that was his problem. The big detective. Well, if he was any bloody good he wouldn't be sitting out his days in a seaside town where nothing ever happened, he would be in the Special Branch in Belfast or Derry, doing something useful instead of poking his nose into everybody's bloody business. Bastard.

Mullan had visited them soon after they moved up from Belfast, obviously sent to check on the 'UVF man' and his family. The shoulders of his fawn raincoat had been darkened by the rain. Stevie had greeted him stiffly, ushering him quickly into the front room; they had talked for more than an hour with the door closed, and when they finally emerged Stevie had shaken his hand briefly at the front door. Colin had watched from behind the banister rail, wondering who the stranger was. Back in Belfast the only people to visit the house had been Stevie's drinking cronies who were all local hoods with no mystery about them. The tall stranger had intrigued him.

Over the years he had been an occasional visitor. Colin had been introduced to him, shaking his hand respectfully. Shortly after his fourteenth birthday Mullan had taken him to a local junior football team and he had trained with them for a few months until the first match of the season, which he remembered as a cold, misty morning with clouds of hot breath swirling around their faces and more mud than grass underfoot. He had twisted his ankle sometime in the second half, and his calf had been slashed by a stud from the opposing team. Mullan had been watching from the sidelines, well wrapped in his sheepskin coat. Colin hadn't gone back after that first match, and Mullan, to his credit, hadn't tried to force him.

At the front of the town there were a few cars parked facing out to sea, with huddled old people watching the breeze whipping at the tops of the waves. All the shops had their lights on, shining yellow through the windows, and out on the harbour wall a solitary man sat peacefully by his fishing rod. The entire world seemed cold and grey.

Colin walked towards the harbour. He could hear the tinny, buzzing sound of a PA system from that end of the town, the noise whipped ragged by the breeze. Sefton, he thought, preaching on a day like this. A grey man for a grey day.

Sefton always chose the same spot for his preaching, a small, open area down by the harbour which was generally empty of parked cars during the winter. A row of three-storey boarding houses looked down on it, Victorian built but now neat and renovated in their pebble-dashed facades, their windows blanked with gauze curtains. Colin had always associated the houses with old people for some reason. Maybe they would enjoy the regular cacophony outside their front doors.

'I am the way, saith the Lord,' Sefton roared, his voice locked in the swaying rhythms of the preacher. The microphone and loudspeakers distorted his voice. His old Volvo estate was parked behind him, the tail-gate open, the loudspeakers sitting on the roof. He held a Bible open in his hand, his scrawny fingers splayed across it to hold the pages down against the breeze. No one was listening to him. Even the shoppers on the far side of the road hurried past with their heads down, avoiding even a glance in his direction.

'Better not stand there too long, or he might convert you.'

Hutchy, looming up behind him, shifting on his feet against the cold.

'Repent, ye sinner,' Colin said. 'What about you, Hutchy?'

'I'm all right. I'm going up to Sefton's house after this. You should come up.'

'Why?'

'You might see something interesting.'

'Doubt it.'

'Seriously, come up. He's nearly finished, anyhow.'

Sefton was singing now, his voice loud and strident over the hissing backing tape of 'Abide with Me'. The breeze was catching long strands of his hair, tugging them vertically into the air.

'Why does he do that?' Colin asked. 'Nobody listens. He isn't going to save any souls today. Any souls with any sense will be at home beside the fire.'

'He just likes to do it. It's his way of worshipping.'

'Aye, well if you ask me the only thing he's worshipping is that bloody microphone.'

The hymn finished at last and Sefton stood for a moment in silence, his eyes closed in prayer, ridiculously thin and scrawny. Then he closed the Bible with a snap and the sermon was over. Hutchy led Colin down to the estate car.

'Hello, boys,' Sefton called when he saw them. 'Good afternoon to you!' He shook hands with them both and his grip was cold and stringy. 'Did you hear the sermon?'

'A bit of it,' Hutchy said.

'We haven't managed to save you yet, have we, Hutchy?' Sefton always spoke of 'we' when he talked about religion, as if there was a vast and powerful brotherhood of lay preachers.

'Me? Nah! Not my scene!'

'What about you, Colin? Not even a glimmer of hope?'

'No.'

'You're very definite about that.'

'I am.'

Sefton gazed at him for a moment, his eyes wet and bleary from the breeze. 'Look, why don't you come back to my house for a while? Hutchy's coming up. Just for an hour or so?'

Colin shrugged. 'All right. But I have to start work at four.'

'Good man. I'll just load the equipment and then we'll take the car.'

The rain came on heavily before they reached Sefton's house and they were soaked on the short dash from the car to the door. They peeled off their sodden coats in the doorway and Sefton draped them over the banister.

'Mother's away to her sister's house in Coleraine this afternoon,' Sefton commented as he led them into the kitchen. It was warm and stuffy, still with the lingering smell of gas.

'So what's happening?' Colin asked, settling himself on one of the kitchen chairs.

Sefton hovered by the doorway for a moment, hesitating, then said 'Wait here,' before disappearing down the hallway and into a bedroom. Colin looked across at Hutchy, who smiled knowingly.

'He's flipped his lid,' Colin hissed.

'Just you wait and see.'

In a few seconds Sefton was back, carrying a long and awkward package which he placed reverently on the kitchen table. The package consisted of thick black polythene strapped up with black tape. It seemed heavy, judging by the way he was carrying it. He hovered over it for a second, his eyes glistening with excitement, before starting to unwrap the thing. Beneath the polythene was a layer of brown paper which had been stained with oil in places, turning it semi-transparent. Colin leaned forward, curious despite himself to see what it was.

'There you go,' Sefton said at last, stepping back from the table. 'What about that, then?'

Colin looked down at the contents of the package and for a second his heart jumped with fear because there were two rifles lying on the kitchen table and that was serious stuff, more than stealing sweets from a newsagent's shop. His mind began to sweep through all the possible consequences of being caught with two weapons; arrest, trial, jail. God only knew what they'd been used for. They had no right to involve him in this. He looked up at Sefton, who was beaming down as if he had just given birth to twins, then down again at the two guns, and then he began to take in the detail and his panic slowed, relief flooding through him. They were guns, all right, but one was an antiquated double-barrelled shotgun and the other looked like an air-rifle. Both had been well-used. There were other bits and pieces

59

lying in the paper wrapping; a telescopic sight and a clear plastic bag full of red shotgun cartridges, as well as some loose springs and various black metal parts. Hutchy reached over and casually lifted the shotgun, breaking it open without having to look for the catch, obviously familiar with it. He held the muzzle to the light and squinted through the barrel.

'Where'd you get these?' Colin asked.

'These are just the start, Colin,' Sefton replied. 'We're organising. We're going to hit back. These Fenian scum have been walking over us for too long. Now we're taking the fight to them.'

'Do they work?'

'They work, all right.'

'Well,' Hutchy put in, 'we still have to fix the 'scope to the air-rifle yet, that's all.'

'Oh, I see.'

Nutcases, Colin thought, the pair of them, bloody nutcases. An air-rifle without a sight and an antique shotgun and the two of them were going to take on the IRA. Nutcases. He held out his hand for the shotgun.

'Let's have a look.'

The gun was old and well-worn, with spots of brown rust here and there on the barrel and dull patches on the stock where the varnish had rubbed off. And yet. And yet it felt good to heft it in his hands, to squint down the barrel with the narrow butt snug in his shoulder. He felt strong and potent, swivelling the two black muzzles around the room, taking aim on the taps, the window catch, the teapot. On Sefton. A real gun. He hefted it in his hands again, savouring the weight of the thing, before handing it carefully back.

'So what are you going to do?'

'Nothing yet,' Sefton said. 'We're still consolidating. We've got powerful people on our side, Colin, you wouldn't believe it if I told you.' He moved to the window and stood staring out towards the rainy garden. 'We're being sold down the garden path, Colin. We're being sold to Dublin. Just like Kenya, like South Africa. Rhodesia. Like all of Britain's friends, we're being stabbed in the back. My grandfather died on the Somme, Colin. He never asked why or wherefore, never questioned; his country called him and he went. And thousands like him, the flower of Ulster manhood. A whole generation. By heaven, if those men had lived this would be a different country today.' He put his fingers out on to the draining board, where they wriggled like repulsive white crabs. 'In 1914 the UVF joined up en masse and became the 36th Ulster division. The army sent them to the Somme and they were destroyed. We have to take up where they left off. We have to do the job they were never able to do. We have to destroy these Republicans before they destroy us. This is only a start,' he said, waving his hand at the kitchen table, 'a small beginning. But great oaks from little acorns grow, Colin. Great oaks.'

The kitchen was suddenly silent except for the patter of the rain on the window. Hutchy sniffed and rubbed at his nose. Nutcase, Colin thought again. Mad as a bloody hatter. What do I say, for heaven's sake? Good luck?

'Very good. Who's we?'

'We're working on a cell system, for security. I am forming one cell. There are . . . others. And a command structure, known only to myself. I can't divulge the names of the other members at this point.'

'You and Hutchy?'

'Hutchy has volunteered his services.'

'But nobody else?'

'I'm not at liberty to say, Colin. I'm sorry.'

'That's all right.'

Sefton straightened up suddenly and moved to the table, placing his hand dramatically on the air-rifle. 'We need expertise, Colin. I've no knowledge of this kind of thing at all. It's come upon me now and with God's help I'll do what I can but I'm no expert. What we need now is someone with experience, an expert.'

'My da.'

'He's the ideal man.'

'No, he isn't.'

'He's had the experience we need!'

'He's had ten years as a cripple, too, don't forget. He's not the same Stevie Rea who was in the UVF, he's just a nasty, twisted, bitter old git!'

'He could help us,' Sefton persisted. He squatted down in front of Colin, looked earnestly into his eyes, placed a grasping hand gently on his knee. Colin tried not to squirm. 'Even advice. Advice would be invaluable.'

'And you want me to ask him?'

'Yes.' They were a silent tableau for a few moments; Colin sitting uncomfortably on the hard kitchen chair, Sefton squatting down and staring up into his eyes, one hand resting on his thigh and Hutchy peering out of the window through the telescopic sight, apparently bored. For long seconds nothing moved. Colin wanted to flick the bluey-white hand from his leg and stamp it to death on the floor like some poisonous tropical insect. The whole business disgusted him; Sefton, the scrappy guns, the faint smell of kitchen gas. They weren't terrorists, they were plain ordinary weirdos acting out their fantasies, that was all. Suddenly he wanted to do or say anything to get out of the warm, muggy house, to get away into the cold, clean rain, away from Sefton and his veiny, grasping hands. 'All right, I'll ask him. If that's what you want.'

'Good man.'

Move your hand, you bastard, or I'll hit you. Colin fought down the panic which was rising in his throat.

'I knew you'd come around, Colin.' Sefton lifted his hand away, more slowly than was necessary. 'Talk to him soon. Time is short.'

'All right. I will. Okay.'

Sefton stood up and went to the sink again. 'Anyone for tea?' he enquired, smiling benevolently at them.

'No thanks,' Colin said quickly. 'I, ah, promised my ma I'd be home early.'

'Well, if you're sure. What about you, Hutchy?'

'Oh, aye,' said Hutchy, tossing the telescopic sight back on to the table. 'I'll take a cup.'

Outside in the street Colin fought back a churning urge to run. They were mad, the two of them. And Sefton was a queer, no doubt about that. He had seen it in the eyes, in the way the hand lingered on his leg. Sick, really sick. The rain was coming on heavy again and he strode on into it, feeling his jeans becoming damp and sticking to his thighs, cold water from the puddles seeping into his shoes. He walked on, quickly, face up to the sky, glad of the coldness of it and the freshness of the smell.

The Committee Room was on the first floor at the top of the stairs, a long, silent room stinking of tradition. There were three windows along one side which were framed by straight curtains of thick blue velvet, draping right down on to the carpet; at night, when they were drawn, they seemed to absorb all sound in the room. It was the sort of room people automatically lowered their voice in. The wall facing the windows was hung with rows of old framed photographs of past teams and previous members, some faded sepia prints from the early years of the century, others more recent, colour, with odd hairstyles and out of date fashions. Each of the photographs had a small dynotape number in the bottom right hand corner, and all their details were held in a book in the sideboard. There were one hundred and twenty-seven photographs on the wall.

Barry still felt uneasy about the room. Besides himself, only the Committee members and the cleaners were allowed into the room without permission, and even then they had to be accompanied. It was one of those useless traditions the club had cherished over the years, but they wanted it observed and so he observed it. He had a childish fear of being caught in the room with no good reason to be there, which was stupid because he was the manager and could go where he liked; even so, he always felt like an interloper. There was always that tiny frisson of apprehension as he looked up and down the landing outside before letting himself in.

The centrepiece of the room was the French Colonels Table, presented by two visiting French officers who had enjoyed the hospitality of the club in the early Twenties. Their names were engraved on a brass plaque on one of the pedestals. It was the size of a billiard table, massive and solid with a polished walnut top and two great carved pedestals. If the Committee Room was the heart of the club then the table was the soul, for it was the essence of everything the club set out to be; old, dignified, a little ugly to look at but worth a hell of a lot of money, and above all, hidden away and cherished.

Barry walked slowly round the table, letting a finger drift lightly across the beautifully polished top. There were years of polish layered on to it, years of care and attention and respect, so that the deep, dark patina almost obscured the delicate sweep of the grain. Each of the Committee members had their own scarlet baize pad to protect the surface of the table. These were known as 'squares', and were passed from member to member with each year's election. Their corners were worn and tatty from decades of use and on several of them the baize was threadbare but it was a minor tradition that they were never replaced until they actually fell to pieces. Shortly before a meeting they would be laid out on the long sideboard against the back wall with a card nameplate beside each one, and normally there would be at least two or three squares left on the sideboard when the meeting commenced. Barry knew that during the meeting on Thursday evening the top of the sideboard would be empty. They would all be there. All eager. Not one of those placid Sunday afternoon affairs, dragged out for an hour over brandy and cigars and finished with nothing achieved. That evening they were meeting for a purpose and a decision had to be made.

Barry paused by the sideboard, looking up at the photographs of past Captains and Chairmen hung in neat rows on the cream and crimson wallpaper. In 1922 the Chairman had been Mr J. J. McNeill, a dour, Scottish-looking man with bushy eyebrows and a stern expression. I wouldn't have had a chance in your day, Barry thought. You wouldn't have let me near the place.

He already had a fair idea how most of them would vote at the meeting. He had sized them up. You could divide people into two groups, he had found, the bigots, and the non-bigots. The bigots were in the main simple men and their behaviour could be predicted with a good degree of accuracy; because he was a Catholic they would vote against him, no matter what the cost to themselves. The non-bigots would follow the dictates of conscience, and that could take them either way.

The Chairman, Brian Tickell, would vote for him. Tickell was a small, determined man who had made his money in furniture sales, and he was astute enough to realise that the issue could not be forced without pushing the club into the embarrassing glare of public scrutiny. Tickell would put the club first. Geoffrey Hicks and Laurence Miller would vote with him, because they were decent men, and strong enough not to bow to pressure. Simon Fowles, the Treasurer, would vote for him because he had been instrumental in his hiring and would be seen to be tarred with the same brush.

Guy McKay and Alan Geraghty would be against him, McKay especially since he was something big in the Orange Order, and Geraghty because he was weak and McKay would influence him. McKay was big and coarse and got drunk a lot and often drove his two-door Mercedes when he was plastered. When they were first introduced McKay had refused to shake his hand. And then there was Miles Granger, who was a loyalist and a hard-liner but not a bigot, as far as Barry could see. He seemed to be the epitome of the old-fashioned land-owning gentleman, courteous and polite and honest. Barry quite liked him; he had his views and his loyalties but he would never parade them in front of you, never try to rub it in your face. He was perhaps the most intelligent of them all, and he would use his intelligence rather than his gut.

The rest of the Committee he didn't know so well; he had met Colin Shannon only once and had formed no opinion of him, although it was said that he had once been charged with disorderly conduct after a loyalist parade in Omagh; something about climbing a lamppost in a drunken attempt to remove a tricolour hanging from the top. Peter Weaver seemed a decent enough chap, but he was in his late sixties and was really past caring; he would be easily influenced by whichever side was the strongest.

Which left the Secretary, Dennis King, who had originally warned Barry of the impending moves. King was a good and straight man and had been behind Barry's appointment from the start, and he would oppose dismissal as a matter of principle. He was a doctor of some sort, and he was always immaculately dressed in the most expensive clothes but he never spoke down to you. He had taken Barry to one side nine days before and told him of the situation in calm but grave tones. 'They want you out, Barry,' he had said. 'There aren't many of them but there are enough to make a noise, and they're going to make as much noise as they can.'

'What reasons are they giving?'

'Reasons?'

'Usually they have lots of reasons for getting rid of the taig.' He spat the last word out, not bothering to hide his bitterness. King had nodded slowly, smoothing his hand over his neat grey hair.

'Well, I'll not lie to you, they've brought up a great variety of points. They're pointing at your background, mainly. You're from the Bogside. As far as they're concerned anyone from the Bogside comes under the general umbrella of IRA supporter. Now I know that's not fair but it's the way their minds work. And what they're saying is that with the proportion of the club membership belonging to the Security Forces in some state or form it would be dangerous to allow someone who may have Republican connections to work in the place.'

'And what do you say, Mr King?'

'I don't think the way they do, if that's what you

mean,' King replied, smiling thinly. 'You're good at your job and I don't think you've any connections of the wrong kind. But the rest of them are frightened, you see, and that's the problem. I would say that seventy per cent of the membership have relatives in the police or the UDR, and they have to think carefully about everything they do. The last thing they want is someone in the club spotting for the terrorists.'

King had been very decent about the whole thing; it had embarrassed him. The civilised society he had believed himself a part of had suddenly reared up and shown its pagan, primitive heart. Barry walked over to the centre window and gazed out at the course, watching the small groups of brightly-coloured people striding to and fro across the fairways. He had never played golf. It seemed a very clean game, very neat. Lots of little coloured markers set out on the tees, the delicate black and white poles in the greens, the little red flags fluttering in the breeze. He had never played golf because he had never moved in those circles; his family and friends had never had enough spare money to spend on fees and clubs and clothes and leisurely living. He hadn't been so privileged.

All his life he had tried not to let himself become bitter, because he had seen all too often how it had destroyed his friends, eating at them and wasting them until all the other parts of their lives dropped away and there was only the bitterness left. And that way led to prison or the grave. But it was hard, sometimes, not to want to strike back, somehow, anyhow. When he was eighteen it had seemed that there were no jobs anywhere in the city; everything he tried seemed to fail, as soon

70

as they saw the name and the address. Roman Catholic. Fenian. The other sort. Dirty people, don't go near them. It was like a wall built up around them to keep them from the real world, and no matter how often you kept banging your head off it you would never break through. It had beaten some of his friends. Sean McVey had joined the IRA and the army had shot him dead in a riot. Gerry O'Brien was killed by his own bomb. Drew Hurley spent three years in prison for armed robbery and had come out a changed man, hardened and cruel and bitter. They had given in to their anger and it had destroyed them.

It was just a matter, he thought, of never generalising about people. People were all different. All Protestants didn't smell, and all Catholics didn't have eyes too close together. Not all loyalists were in the UVF, and not all Catholics were IRA men. Take people as you find them, that was the rule. If they are bastards, then hate them, but only because of what they are, and not what they come from.

He walked back to the door again, stopping to straighten a photograph of the Connor Cup team of 1926. No point worrying about it too much, he was thinking, I'll find out soon enough. Besides, there was nothing they could really do, in law; they couldn't just dismiss him because he was a Catholic, they would have to find some fault with his work and he knew that was impossible. And even if they did dismiss him out of hand there were all sorts of avenues open to him for redress, and he would always get the job back. But what sort of job would it be then, knowing that your employers didn't want you? Would it be worth fighting that particular battle? Was anything worth all that trouble? He cast a last, rueful glance around the room then closed the door gently behind him.

When Colin arrived home his father was in the hallway preparing for one of his walks. He walked now and again to ease his temper. Generally he went down to the strand, which was about half a mile away, and walked along the hard sand near the sea. He had to bring a stick in case his leg became too tired on the way back, and the stick often sank into the sand, and he would return in a worse temper than before.

'Hi,' Colin said, squeezing past his father who was trying to zip up his old waterproof.

'Where were you?'

'Just messing about. With Hutchy.'

Stevie gnawed at his lip for a moment, nodding to himself. Colin sensed that he wanted to say something else and that it might be an apology. He didn't want him to say anything. It was easy to live with him as a bad tempered tyrant; to admit his humanity would make it worse, would entitle him to pity. Stevie was standing with his shoulders slightly stooped and both hands on the ends of the zip and his eyebrows raised and his forehead furrowed, making him look old. He looked like a father. 'Right,' he muttered, turning back to the zip.

'How's Mum?'

'She's asleep.'

'Oh.'

Stevie straightened up and tugged the zip upwards, sealing the jacket. He pulled his walking stick from the hallstand. 'I'm away for a walk,' he said. 'I'll be back soon.'

Colin stood awkwardly at the far end of the hallway, watching him, wondering whether to ask him or not. This would be a good time because Stevie seemed to be in good form and it probably wouldn't last, and he had promised Hutchy and Sefton that he would ask. On the other hand, you never knew how the old bastard would react.

'Is there anything you want?' Stevie asked, his voice a little harder.

'Ah . . . yes, there is.'

'Well?'

'Well . . . remember when we lived in Belfast? When you were in the UVF?'

Stevie's eyes narrowed because that name had not been mentioned in the family for ten years and Colin wondered if he was wise to go on but he had started and there was no point going back. Stevie was interested now and his attention was suddenly focused.

'What about it?'

'There's a fellow starting up something like that. In the town. He's only just getting going, you know, but

74

he says he has contacts and he was saying that he needs all the help he can get and – '

'And you thought of me?'

'Well, you've got a lot of experience – '

'That's true.' Stevie moved suddenly closer, within arm's reach, stooping slightly to stare into Colin's face. Colin stared back, trying to gauge the reaction, suspecting that something was wrong but not sure what or why. 'Who is this character?'

'Sefton – '

'The preacher?'

'Aye.'

'And what sort of help does he want, exactly?' There was a gleam in the old man's eyes but it didn't look pleasant and Colin was suddenly worried. He made to step back and knocked into the door post. 'Wants advice, does he? Experience? How to organise, how to plan, is that what he wants, is it? How to use a gun, maybe, does he want a bit of help with that, does he? Aye, I could help him there, all right.' He was leaning forward and down, breathing almost into Colin's face, his voice growing steadily louder. Little beads of spittle were bouncing and dancing on his lower lip. Colin remembered times when he was a kid and his father had beaten him, and was frightened. 'Maybe he wants more than information, eh? Maybe more than advice, maybe he wants me to join the group, would that be it? Oh, I'd be an asset, wouldn't I? Maybe he'd want me to help in the jobs. Maybe he'd want me to take part in a few of them; nothing serious, not an old man like me, not at first anyway. Maybe a few robberies. Or kneecappings.

Or maybe he wants me to kill someone for him, is that it?'

He was almost shouting but not quite and there was a terrible control about him and for the first time in his life Colin was terrified of his father. This was a side he had never seen before. This was something new and horrible, the eyes still and dead and cold and the mouth hanging slightly open. Now he could understand why people had once feared him. Colin felt the door post hard in his back. He felt sweat in his palms. Suddenly the hallway was too small and too gloomy and Stevie could do anything to him and he would never escape. He tried to think of something to say, then there was a blur of colour and a massive crack and he felt his head snap sideways as his father's open hand smashed across his cheek.

'Now you listen to me, son!' he hissed, jabbing his forefinger at him. 'Are you listening?'

'Yes!'

'Well get this into your thick skull. Don't you ever get involved with any organisation, ever, is that clear? You stay away from that fellow Sefton, all right? That means right out of his way! And if I hear that you've been hanging around with him, so help me God I'll kill you myself! You hear me?'

Colin nodded frantically.

'Good.'

Suddenly Stevie's hand moved again and Colin felt another massive, stinging impact on the side of his face, this time knocking his head back against the door post. He dropped to his knees, clutching his face, cringing away from the expected kick. Stevie looked down at him for a moment, then quickly stalked down the hall and out the front door, banging it hard behind him.

He arrived at work at five past four and there were some strange looks but no one mentioned anything so he nipped into the toilet as soon as he could and examined his face in the mirror. His eye wasn't blackened which was a small mercy but there was a big blue bruise developing over the left cheekbone and the cut on his lip was still dark and crusty. He wiped at the cut with a damp paper towel as best he could, trying to avoid opening it again, then splashed cold water on his face.

The initial shock at the violence of his father's reaction had given way to hurt which in turn had given way to anger, and now he was raging with self-justification and shame. Stevie had no right to hit him like that. That was no way for a father to hit a son. He could have broken his jaw. He was nothing but a stupid, nasty, vicious old git, so fuck him, fuck him and his orders! His twisted bloody leg had made him bitter so he took it out on his family! Bastard.

The bar was quiet and he served a few drinks and Ernie sent him down to the store for two bottles of vodka, and when he came back Mullan was standing at the bar. The policeman's eyes widened as he took in Colin's face.

'What the hell happened to you?' he said incredulously.

'I fell.'

Ernie laughed under his breath. 'Fell against a good slap in the head, if you ask me.'

'Aye, well, nobody did.'

'Fair enough.'

'What did happen to you?' Mullan persisted.

'I fell, all right?'

'Ernie, could you spare him for five minutes, do you think?' Mullan asked.

'Sure.'

'Good. Right, young man, come you with me.'

'Why?'

'Just do it!'

Colin followed him outside. It was already dark and the air was sharp with the cold. Their breath showed cloudy in the security lights. Colin walked sullenly beside the taller man, their feet scrunching on the gravel drive.

'Your father phoned me,' Mullan began.

'He had no right – '

'He had every right! He's your father. Now shut up and listen!'

They walked across the car park, Colin walking quickly by the policeman's side, saying nothing but somehow reminded of the last walk to the gallows. The car park was almost empty, the few remaining cars gleaming like giant, watching beetles in the light of the high-powered security lamps. Mullan walked to the far corner and stopped in a pool of white light cast by one of the lamps. Colin stopped a few paces from him. There was a broken wooden tee on the tarmac and he started to roll it to and fro under his foot.

'Now look,' Mullan began, thrusting his hands deep into his trouser pockets. 'I've known your father for some time now. We've done each other a few favours. He asked me to talk to you tonight.'

'Hah! That's a laugh! Getting a stranger to do what he can't do himself?'

'He told me he hit you. It must have been some dunt he gave you, judging by your face.'

'Well, it smarted, I can tell you that!'

'Calm down, Colin, he's worried about you, that's all. He said you were getting into the wrong company.'

'Did he?'

'Yes. He didn't say who it was. Although I've probably got a fair idea.'

'Oh aye? Who would that be, then?'

'I'm not here to make accusations.'

'That'll be the first time he's worried about anything in his life, well. He's nothing but an arrogant old fool who hasn't a thought for anyone other than himself!'

There was a silence for a while as Mullan gathered his thoughts but it was an angry silence and Colin could feel the other man's annoyance building. Colin mustered his own rage to help him argue back. Mullan had no right talking to him like this. Who did he think he was?

'Now you listen to me – ' Mullan began grasping at the top of Colin's arm but Colin jerked away and stepped quickly back a few steps.

'No, you listen to me! What right do you have to interfere in our lives? Every time I turn round you're on my back about something! Why'd you tell my mother that I applied to join the police? Why'd you tell her?'

'I had to tell her. If you'd got any further they would have written to your parents, anyway – '

'You might at least have gone back to her and told her I didn't get in!'

Mullan blinked a few times, frowned slightly, paused.

'That's neither here nor there,' he snapped, but Colin could see by the shadow in his face that the point had hit home.

'Aye! You forgot to tell her, didn't you! And she spent three months waiting to hear some good news, hoping I'd get in! You put her through that, nobody else! It's your fault!'

The anger was bouncing inside him now and he felt his mind tossing up other reasons, other justifications, and another thing, it said, and another thing, but then Mullan recovered quickly from his brief flash of weakness and he grabbed Colin by the shoulder, his fingers stiff and steely. He swung him round and slapped him quickly across the face, not as hard as Stevie had done, but hard enough, and on the already tender bruise. Colin cried out and made to fall but Mullan held him up.

'Now you listen to me, son. Let's get back to the point of our little chat. Your da is concerned about you because he's lived a lot longer than you have and he's already been on the road you're looking down and he knows where it leads to! So do I, for that matter, because if you carry on the way you're going it'll be me who'll be taking your statement down at the station. I'll be the one who'll have to listen to your bawling and crying because you can't sleep with your conscience screaming at you. Or I'll be the one who has to drag your body out of some hedge and count the holes and take it to the morgue! Now there's a lot of people who'll go down that road and I don't give a fiddler's frig if they kill themselves or land themselves in jail, because they're useless wasting bastards. But you're not like that, son, you're intelligent, you've got a brain, you've got a chance in this world! Don't throw it away! That's what your da is worried about!'

'He's nothing but an old criminal who can't scare people any more – '

Mullan's hand shot out and grabbed Colin by the shirt front and Colin felt himself being lifted upwards, the seams of the sleeves tightening into his armpits.

'Your father's a better man than you'll ever know, son,' Mullan said quietly. 'And if you don't know that, then you don't know him very well.' He let go of the shirt and Colin fell backwards on to the damp tarmac. The light was behind Mullan's head and the breath swirling round him glowed like some demonic halo. 'Now stay out of trouble! For your own sake!'

When he got back into the bar Ernie James was openly leering at him. 'Where's Mullan?' he asked.

'Gone home.'

'You in trouble with the law already? At your age?'

'Bugger off, Ernie, would you?' The back of his shirt was soiled and dirty and his face was aching. And worse than that, his pride was hurt. Barry Kelly beckoned him discreetly into his office.

'Are you all right, Colin?'

'Aye. No problems.'

'You're sure? If you're in any kind of trouble, maybe we could help you.'

'No. Thanks, but there's no trouble. It's kind of a . . . family thing, you know.' He was embarrassed by the obvious kindness. He stared down at the rough oatmeal tweed of the carpet, fixing his eyes on a small blue inkstain near the leg of the desk.

'Well. If you're sure.' Barry reached into one of the desk drawers and pulled out a bunch of keys. He tossed them to Colin.

'White chest of drawers in my room, second drawer down, you'll find a clean shirt. Lock the door again after you.'

Colin felt his cheeks flush. 'Thanks,' he said.

'Can't have you working in that state, now, can we? You'd only frighten the customers. And make sure I get it back washed and ironed, all right?'

There were cliffs near the town, not very high cliffs, but steep, falling down to clumps of cold black rocks, darkened by the sea at high tide. Along the top a path led back into the town, with a high wall on one side sealing off the convent, and there were wooden benches at the wider spots where you could sit and stare out at the perfect hard line of the horizon. The clifftops had always seemed to Colin to be civilised and neat, while below the path everything was wild, uncontrolled and unrestrained; the sea smashed against the containing land like a trapped animal against a cage, the wind tugged and pulled at you as though trying to topple you off the narrow path, the cold made your cheeks sting. There were places where you could climb down on to the rocks, and when the tide was out Colin often picked his way out along the rubble of stones to where the seaweed swayed in the deeper water. He would go right out to the last rock and squat down and look out at the distant horizon, knowing the depth of the water and the distance of the sea. You felt you were on the edge of something, when you sat there, as if there was only you and the sea and you understood each other. It was a place you could only get to when the sea was calm, and it was almost a thrill to realise that you would drown there in bad weather, or die with your head split open on the rocks.

Once he had found a dead seal lying stupid and ugly across a small rock pool. Its head had been pulped against the rocks, leaving it almost unrecognisable, like some dead creature from outer space. He had stood over it with Hutchy, wanting to make fun of it and yet aware that it had recently been a living, breathing, warm-blooded creature and that it deserved better than the jokes of boys. It was the biggest thing he had ever seen dead. They called the cleft of rocks it had come to rest in 'Seal Bay' ever since. When they went back a day later the body had gone, vanished without a trace.

Colin walked out to the edge of the path, and looked down at the rock pool where the body had lain. Five, six years ago, perhaps? The rocks had not changed, the pool was still there, the dark stone was still encrusted with small white shells. The seal would be nothing now, returned to the sea, broken down into elements and merged into everything else. That was the way things worked. You existed, you died, and you disappeared. And that was that.

He pushed gently at the tender skin on his cheek, wincing at the sudden pain. The bruise had turned a dirty, pasty yellow until it looked like some awful dis-ease splashed across his face. He hadn't said a word to Stevie since that afternoon, and Stevie had barely looked in his direction. Angie had picked up the vibes, but had said nothing; probably she had guessed. She didn't stand up to the old man half enough, Colin thought. He had stayed out of the house as much as he could to avoid the irritation of the whole thing. What did it matter, in any case? What did it matter who he spent his time with, as long as he stayed out of trouble? Nobody gave him credit for any self-control, that was the problem. Nobody trusted him. Screw them all, he thought.

He considered climbing down and scrambling out along the rocks but the sea was choppy and the tide was coming in, so he turned instead and walked back along the path towards the town. He wondered for the hundredth time what the convent was like behind the wall. The building itself was plain enough; it could be seen from most parts of the town, sitting high and clean on the headland. But what was it like beyond the wall? Was it neat or untidy? Did they have lawns, or was it all concrete? The walls went all the way around, even on the far side, next to the road, and there were tall wooden gates which were seldom opened. Only the chosen few were allowed in. Maybe that's what heaven is like, Colin reflected; a massive convent with high walls all around. And no admittance to the likes of me.

He walked down off the path and into the town and turned right, heading along the Coleraine Road, going home but not really wanting to. He was to start work at four and it was only just after one and there were three hours to kill. Water from the puddles was seeping into his shoe through a crack in the sole and his sock was damp and clammy, but somehow he felt that it fitted his mood. He was outside the butcher's shop when Sefton pulled up in his car, hooting the horn to get his attention. Hutchy was sitting in the passenger seat. Colin stood and watched as Sefton stretched back and opened the back door for him, and he considered ignoring the offer, but then again, he was bored and it was something to do.

'Hello, Colin,' Sefton said. 'We're going out for a wee drive. You want to come with us?'

'Might as well.'

'Good man.'

The car smelled of peppermint. There were stickers in the windows about the wages of sin being death, and the coming of the Lord being nigh. Hutchy leaned round in the seat and grinned at him.

'What about you?' he asked cheerfully.

'How come you're always so bloody happy these days, Hutchy?'

'How come you're always so pissed off? And who kicked you in the face?'

'I fell.'

'Against somebody's boot?'

Sefton was craning round now, trying to see what they were talking about. 'Just you keep your eyes on the road,' Colin told him. Sefton glanced up into the rear-view mirror and examined his face in it.

'That's a bad bruise,' he said.

'It's not too bad now.'

'What happened?'

'I asked my da if he would help. He went buck mad. Tried to beat the living daylights out of me.'

Hutchy looked shocked. 'What for?' he asked.

'For getting involved in things I shouldn't.'

'Sure he was in the UDA, wasn't he? Where's his problem?'

'UVF, Hutchy.'

'Same difference.' He seemed affronted by the hypocrisy of it. 'Why should he mind you following in his footsteps?'

'You tell me.'

Sefton drove very badly. He clashed the gears often, and seemed to clasp the steering wheel too tightly for comfort.

'So where are we going to?' Colin asked.

'Sightseeing,' Hutchy replied, tapping the side of his nose wisely. He grinned stupidly. 'Up in the forest.'

'I have to be at work by four o'clock, don't forget.'

'Relax, would you, for God's sake.'

They drove into Coleraine and out the far side, heading north-west into the country. It was bleak country, too; rolling hills stretching off inland, smeared with dark patches of pine forest, and flat windswept land to seaward, with the occasional trees bent and stunted by the constant wind. Up on the headland was the gaunt ruin of Downhill House, once the residence of the Bishop of Derry but since the 1700s merely a giant shell of empty windows.

Hutchy and Sefton were discussing something in the front but Colin ignored them, lying back in the seat and letting his mind wander, soothed by the constant dull roar of the engine. It was a terrible state of affairs when you didn't even want to go back to your own home, he was thinking. When no one would speak either to you or for you.

'Colin?' Sefton asked. 'Do you know a fellow called Kelly who's working at the golf club?'

'Barry Kelly?'

'That's him.'

'Aye, I know him. He's the manager.'

'The word is that he's a bad boy.'

'A what?'

'I've heard tell that he's involved with the Provisionals. Rumours going around, you know, only rumours, but there's no smoke without fire, that's what I always say.'

'Nah, he's not into anything like that.'

'How do you know?' Hutchy asked, swinging round in the seat again.

'He's a decent bloke. Wherever you're getting your rumours from, I think they're wrong.'

'He's from the Bogside,' Sefton said. 'He grew up among the scum. And now he's trying to get out of their ghetto.'

Sefton's voice was sharpened with the hatred. He had no call to talk like that about Kelly and Colin was about to bring up the story of the borrowed shirt when he thought that it might not be a good idea to be seen to be too close to him. And anyway, none of what these two lunatics thought was of the slightest importance. He turned back to the dark, brooding countryside slipping past outside.

'You could do us a favour,' Sefton said after a while. 'You could keep an eye on him.'

'Why?'

'Just in case he does anything suspicious.'

'No.'

'It might be very important, Colin.'

'Look what happened to me the last time I did you a

favour! I nearly got a broken cheekbone! No more bloody favours!'

They were on the main road which eventually led down to Magilligan Strand and round the bottom of the Binvenagh Cliffs. The road twisted around the foot of the cliffs and from the road you could see the tiny waterfalls which sometimes froze solid in winter, leaving white ice-trails down the clefts in the rock. Before they reached the bottom of the hill Sefton indicated and swung left off the main road and they began to move uphill.

'What's up here?' Colin asked.

'There's a beautiful view up here, absolutely beautiful,' Sefton said. 'Of course, this maybe isn't the best sort of weather for it. You really need a sunny day. But it should be spectacular.'

He was acting strangely, more tense and jerky than usual. He seemed nervous, Colin thought. Hutchy was sitting calmly in the front seat with his head slightly lowered, peering out of the windscreen at the narrow road ahead. They were travelling across the top of the mountain, between two low dry-stone walls, and on each side was flat bogland stretching out to the grey horizon. Here and there were black heaps of freshly-cut turf standing over the dark scars of the cutting.

'We're meeting someone up here, Colin,' Sefton explained. 'His name is Davidson. That's all you need to know.'

'Meeting him? Why up here?'

'Just wait and see,' Hutchy said, rubbing his big hands together in excitement.

Sefton swung right, then right again, then they were

slowing down and pulling into a tarmac'd car park surrounded by stone walls. The ground sloped gently down to the edge of the cliff then dropped abruptly into nothing; laid out before them in the distance was the massive promontory of Magilligan Point, poking out into Lough Foyle, with the grey sea foaming in lines along the broad sandy Atlantic beaches. Across the Lough were the shores of Donegal, soft rolling hills dotted with tiny white houses and taller purple mountains behind. The sky was low and grey and cloudy, heavy-looking, as though about to burst.

Sefton wrenched on the handbrake and switched off the engine and they sat for a moment in the sudden creaking silence, staring out of the windscreen at the view. I suppose this is why the tourists come, Colin thought. Good luck to them. I wouldn't travel too far for this.

'He's not here,' Hutchy said, stating the obvious.

'He'll be here.'

'Who is he?' Colin asked.

'I don't want you to say anything when he does arrive, Colin. We're in the middle of a wee business deal . . . don't ask any questions when he's here. All right?'

There was the sound of a car approaching and then a flashy looking Escort bumped down to a halt beside them. Sefton licked quickly at his lips.

'Here he is,' Hutchy said cheerfully, opening the door.

'No, Hutchy, wait,' said Sefton, snatching at Hutchy's arm. 'Let me handle it.'

'Bollocks,' Hutchy replied, shaking off the arm and getting out.

There was only one man in the other car and he was

staring placidly out towards Donegal, not even glancing in their direction. Hutchy lumbered up to the driver's window and knocked on it.

'Are you Davidson?' he asked. The other man looked round slowly, as if a five-year-old had asked a stupid question. He was a heavy-looking fellow with longish fair hair, all neatly combed back from his face. He shifted in the seat and wound down the window.

'Are you Sefton?'

Hutchy jerked a thumb at the older man. 'He is.' Davidson's eyes narrowed, sweeping quickly up and down Sefton's narrow figure. He nodded slowly, then heaved himself out of the car and walked slowly round to the boot. A large beer-belly protruded from his open leather jacket and he wore polished tan cowboy boots with his jeans out over them. Hutchy followed him around to the back of the car, but Sefton stood by his own car, his face tense and white, his hands hanging loosely by his side. Colin noticed that they were clenching and reclenching into tight white fists.

Davidson reached into the boot and withdrew a large package made from a taped-up fertiliser bag. He held it out to Hutchy, who took it eagerly. It seemed heavy.

'Is that it, then?' Hutchy asked.

'What do you want, a fucking receipt?'

They stood quietly motionless for a moment, then Davidson shrugged and eased himself back into the car. He started the engine and almost at the same time began to reverse, not at top speed but more quickly than was normal. Sefton jerked, as though the sudden movement had shocked him into wakefulness, and hurried round to his own side of the car.

'Hurry up, Hutchy,' he called, breathlessly. 'Let's get out of here.'

It was the kind of excitement that comes after a period of tension, the racing, pounding, screaming madness which just says: run. Sefton drove like a lunatic, out on to the road with the car sliding almost into the ditch, then accelerating away towards the forest. Hutchy had the package across his knees, and he whooped with excitement. Sefton was grinning. Colin fell about in the back seat, trying to stay upright. There was that old, guilty sinking feeling in his stomach; he had an idea what was in the bag and he didn't like it.

Sefton braked hard and turned off the narrow road, on to a track leading into the forest. The car bumped and bounced along the muddy, rutted surface with the fir trees looming up on each side, the sky dwindling to a broad strip of grey between them. They came to a clearing where the track forked, then ended, and Sefton slowed down and stopped in the centre of it. He pulled the handbrake on and slapped at the steering wheel, grinning hugely.

'I thought we were going to stash them right away?' Hutchy asked, suspiciously.

'No. We'll check them here.'

'But you said – '

'I know what I said! Now give me that bag!' He switched off the engine and looked across at Hutchy, who had both his arms around the package. Hutchy stared back, looking as though he might argue, then he suddenly tossed the package to Sefton.

'All right. You're the boss.'

They had to use an old screwdriver which Sefton

found in the boot to rip open the binding. Hutchy worked at it on the bonnet of the car, while Sefton looked on, and Colin hovered uncertainly in the background. He was frightened now. These idiots were into something serious, and this was the middle of the bloody countryside, and anyone could be out there watching. He stared around the clearing, his arms folded against the cold, wishing he had worn his pullover under his jacket. Around the edge of the clearing were small heaps of domestic rubbish, spilled from the shreds of old black binliners and spread untidily on the muddy grass. The trees on the edge of the forest stood behind the litter in a dump, silent line, while behind them the rows of straight trunks led off into the darkness. There was almost complete silence, except for the soft hiss of the pine needles rubbing in the breeze and Hutchy's grunts as he poked and pulled at the strong tape. Colin felt naked and vulnerable, as though he were standing in a theatre in front of hundreds of people. As though each of the fir trees was a living, breathing witness.

'That's it!' Sefton said, rubbing his hands. Hutchy ripped apart some of the fertiliser bag, then reached in and tugged out a thick black object which did not seem to take on a shape until he held it up above his head and waved it in the air and then Colin realised it was a machine-gun. Suddenly he felt a great swooping emptiness falling through his stomach. Jesus, he thought, Jesus Christ, I need to get away from this. None of it seemed real; the gun, the car, the silent, breathing forest. He was caught up in some low-quality thriller and there was a camera somewhere, and soon they would call 'Cut'.

Now Sefton had a pistol in his hands, turning it this way and that, not sure what to do with it.

'You bastards!' Colin shouted suddenly. The sound of his voice was amplified by the stillness, and Hutchy seemed to duck slightly. Sefton stiffened, and the two of them froze awkwardly with the guns in their hands.

'What did you bring me for? I don't want to get involved in this!'

'Calm down, Colin – ' Sefton began.

'Fuck you! What are you going to do with those?'

'I told you often enough!'

'You're going to kill people!'

'Only if we have to.'

'Bollocks! You brought me along just to get me involved, that's all! Well, it won't work. Fuck you and your war!'

Hutchy had been ambling closer and all of a sudden he was right up against him with the machine-gun pointed at his throat and the threat coming out of him in waves. Colin swallowed, and felt the cold snout of the gun pushing at his Adam's apple. Hutchy was holding him by his upper arm, fingers tight, hurting.

'Colin. You're in. Or you're out. That's all there is to it.' He pushed the gun hard against his neck. 'Understand?'

'What are you doing, Hutchy?' Colin pleaded softly. 'What are you fucking well doing?'

'It's a war. And people get hurt in wars. Do you want those bastards to win?'

'You and me were going to be in the police, Hutchy!'

'You've got to fight them. One way or another.'

This is not my mate, Colin kept thinking, this is not my mate. This is not the friend I robbed the sweet shop with. He looked across at Sefton who was watching from the car, still holding the pistol loosely in his hands. His face was calm and interested. What have you done to my mate, Colin thought, feeling the anger surging through him, giving him strength. What the hell did you do to him? Suddenly the fear was all gone and all his actions seemed open and clear-cut and it seemed that every detail of the scene was rushing into his head, as though his eyes were suddenly twice as strong and his mind was twice as broad. He shook his arm once and broke free of Hutchy's grip with a gesture of irritation and stepped back, out of his grasp. Hutchy stood where he was, his mouth slightly open, his eyes wide and surprised. He gestured with the gun again, but it was a loose, incoherent movement and all the threat was gone.

'Fuck off, Hutchy, it's me you're talking to here, remember.'

'We'd better not hang around too long,' Sefton said.

'Well, I'm not going back with you,' Colin announced.

'Don't be silly, Colin. You can't walk anywhere from here. It's miles to the nearest town.'

'You can drop me at the first bus-stop, then. I'm not going through a town with you two and that stuff.' He nodded at the opened package.

'I thought you would have understood, Colin,' said Sefton sadly.

'We all make mistakes, don't we?'

They dropped him at a bus-stop outside Articlave and he waited twenty-five minutes for a bus to Coleraine. From there he took another back home. All the way back he sat staring out of the window, now and again

94

resting his forehead against the trembling, vibrating glass, trying to make his mind function. His brain was clogged with fear. I could go to prison for this, he kept thinking. I could go to prison. Those were real guns, and God only knew who Davidson was. But far worse than that was the thought of what the two idiots might do with them. You didn't use guns to cut the grass, or sew on buttons. They were for killing with. Just outside Coleraine the rain came on and the windscreen wipers began to thump backwards and forwards across the glass, and Colin found his head full of the one word, repeated constantly with each rhythmic, squeaking movement of the wiper arm; fun–eral, fun–eral, fun–eral, fun–eral. Someone was going to die. They were going to kill a person. This was real. This was not a TV show.

The Committee meeting commenced at eight o'clock sharp on Thursday evening. Barry hung around the kitchen and the lounge, trying to keep out of the way of the main hall in order to avoid meeting any of the members on their way upstairs. It was a very slack night with only two tables booked in the restaurant, and the kitchen staff were sitting round a small table in the back store, sipping tea and gossiping. He sat with them for a while and chatted to the chef, but the conversation was brief and flat and ten minutes later he couldn't remember what he had said.

Ernie James and Colin Rea were on duty in the bar, which was also empty. The curtains were not drawn and there was nothing in the windows but the reflection of the bar and a pool of light on the gravel outside. Barry stood behind the bar for a long while and stared out at his reflection in the polished glass, trying to get his thoughts in order. He would have preferred a busy night, with something to do, rather than this dull, silent waiting. Even the piped music machine was broken.

'Pull those curtains, Colin, would you?' he said at last, watching until the blue velvet swallowed up his reflection.

'When do you think they'll be finished, boss?' asked Ernie James.

'God knows,' Barry replied. He glanced up at the ceiling, as though the meeting going on upstairs might be making a visible sign.

'Where were you born, Ernie?' he asked after a moment.

'I'm a Derry man, boss.'

'Whereabouts?'

'The Waterside.'

Barry smiled. 'Good Protestant country.'

'Aye, it is, aye.'

'I'm from the Bogside, myself.'

'Aye.'

'Don't suppose you'd know it all that well, would you?'

Ernie had been making himself busy stocking the splits and mixers but now he stopped and eased himself up from the half-empty crate. He rubbed his back a little as he straightened. 'Oh, I've some good friends from the Bog,' he said. 'Don't see them that often, but they're good people.'

Barry leaned back against the worktop and folded his arms. 'What's it all about, Ernie?' he asked. 'What is it all about? I mean, ever since I was a young lad it's been the same story, the same aggravation. We used to get hassled in the streets all the time, you know. First the police. Then the Army arrived, and eventually they were at it, too. Always getting stopped and searched and asked your name and where you were going and what you were doing. How old are you, Ernie?'

'Oh, too old. Well past it.'

'You must be in your forties, anyway, would that be right?'

'Round about that, aye.'

'Well, you must remember what it was like, before all this started? I can just remember it. The one thing I can remember is that nobody gave a fiddler's frig what religion you were, and you could go anywhere, anywhere at all, and no one would touch you. Do you not remember that?'

'Aye,' Ernie said, nodding slowly. 'We used to celebrate the twelfth of July and all your lot would be out round the bonfires too, singing and dancing like the rest of us.' He smiled at some private memory. 'Changed times, boss, changed times.'

'You're telling me.'

The evening dragged like no other evening. At nine o'clock a small party of seven came in and had a few drinks in a corner of the lounge, but the big room was too empty and their laughter echoed and they left again shortly after ten. Silence settled on the lounge again.

There was little chance of custom after that so Barry sat down in the lounge with the two barmen and they chatted for a while, leaning back in the plush upholstery. Ernie lit a cigarette and blew smoke into the air. Colin sat quietly, touching now and again at the bruise on his face. He was healing up quickly; another two or three days and there would be nothing there to show for it.

That was a bad thing to do, Barry thought, hitting a young lad like that, no matter what the reason. Especially a big fellow like Mullan. He had sensed that something was wrong and had been about to follow the two of them into the car park when Ernie James had gently restrained him. Family trouble, he said. You're better staying out of it. Which was probably true. But then again, he was the manager and he had an obligation to his staff to look after them and he felt that he had in some way failed the lad.

Of course the worry was that Colin would get into trouble with the police. You always had to watch that with the younger staff. When he had managed the River Lodge in Derry most of his barmen had had criminal records of some sort. It hadn't bothered him particularly, so long as they didn't steal from him; besides which, good bar staff wouldn't have looked twice at a place like the River Lodge and you had to make do with what you could get, letting them have time off for court and seeing their probation officer and so on. Young Colin wasn't like that, though; it would be a shame to see him go the same way.

At around half-past ten there was a bubble of conversation from the hall and the clumping of feet down the stairs and the meeting was obviously over. The two barmen nipped behind the bar. Barry hovered at the door of the lounge, listening. The talk was fast and heated, by the sound of it; some of the voices sounded indignant and offended, others just tired. Barry waited until he heard the distant clunk of car doors slamming closed before easing out into the hallway. Dennis King was just coming down the stairs, a small document case in his hand. He looked exhausted.

'Oh, Barry,' he said, coming to the foot of the stairs. He had the air of a man who had been caught sneaking out. 'Ah . . . let's go into your office, shall we?'

I don't want to hear this, Barry thought desperately, I'm not a brave man, I don't carry these things well. I like this job. I might not get another. Judging by the atmosphere, all was not well. And just when I was beginning to get used to this little office. He sat down behind his desk and King eased himself into the armchair by the side of it and they sat for a moment, looking at each other.

'Well, Barry,' King said heavily, 'Looks like you're staying.'

Thank you, Jesus, Mary and Joseph, I will go to Mass, I promise. Barry clenched his fists under the desk in a tense, shaking relief.

'Although, let me tell you, I wouldn't like to have another Committee meeting like that for a while. I've never seen anything like it.' He looked tired and drawn, pinching the bridge of his nose with his thumb and forefinger. 'The knives were out tonight, all right. McKay and Geraghty were out for blood, yours, or anyone else who stood in their way, they didn't care.'

'What were they saying?'

'Well, they were making the case almost entirely on security grounds. They went on about the number of policemen who play here regularly, and so forth. Their argument is that you would be a security risk.'

'But that's ridiculous!'

'You know that and I know that. But they did put a

very convincing case. Now, apparently these two charac-
ters Montgomery and Thompson, who started the whole
thing, had dug into your background in some depth.
You had an uncle who was interned in the Seventies,
apparently. They threw that up.'

'Half my street was interned in the Seventies,' Barry
replied. 'Lots of people were lifted. My uncle Gerry had
been arrested for something stupid in 1959 and it was
still on record, and that was why they interned him.
They let him out in three weeks, for God's sake.'

'I know that. Look, I didn't intend ever telling you
this but Brian Tickell and I had you cleared through the
RUC before we ever offered you the job; Mullan ran a
trace on you for us. They said you were clean, and that
was good enough for us. Now, McKay and Geraghty
weren't aware of that, so we let them make their case
for about an hour, then threw it in on them, and I think
that was what swung it. If the RUC say you're all right,
then you're all right. Or at least, that's how I saw it.
And so did the rest of the Committee, luckily enough.
Anyway, once we'd knocked their chairs from under
them the whole thing descended into raw, naked bigotry,
nothing more.' The old man shook his head sadly. 'I'll
tell you what, Barry, I had my eyes opened tonight. I
heard things I didn't believe I'd ever hear said in a
civilised place like this.'

Barry smiled thinly. 'Welcome to the world, Mr King,'
he said. King nodded again.

'The good work you've done since you came also
stood you in good stead, I should say. No one could
fault you there.'

Barry wanted to ask more questions about who had

said what and so forth, but the old man looked tired and broken and it was getting late.

'You'd best be getting off home, Mr King,' he said. 'Your wife will be worrying about you.'

'Yes, I suppose she will. Are you married, Barry?'

'I was once, long time ago.'

'God, yes, you're living upstairs, I'm sorry, I should have realised.'

'Don't worry about it. I've got that complacent, married look about me, that's what it is. Well, I have now, anyway.'

'Well, the important thing is, you're staying. And they can't put you out now, I don't think. They've exhausted all their avenues, and I really don't believe there's anything else they can try.' He eased himself up from the chair and carefully straightened his jacket. He paused for a second, then looked hard at Barry. 'There's one thing, Barry,' he said carefully. 'Watch out for the personalities involved. McKay especially. He's a nasty piece of work.'

'I will, Mr King, I will. Get you on home now. And thanks for filling me in.'

'You deserve it, Barry. Least I could do.'

Barry walked him out to his car, their feet crunching on the frozen gravel. The car windscreen was already beginning to freeze over. 'You mustn't let this business affect your opinion of the majority of the club, Barry,' King said, as he sorted at his keys. 'Most of them are decent, honest people, like yourself.'

'Most of the world is like that, Mr King. It's the bigots who spoil it.'

'You're right, Barry. You're right, indeed. Well, good-night. Sleep well.'

I will, Mr King, Barry thought as he watched the red tail-lights disappear into the darkness, don't you worry about that, I will all right.

The next evening he drove back to Derry to his brother's big new house on the green slopes overlooking the Foyle. Patrick was throwing an engagement party for his son Brendan and his girlfriend Marie, but it was as much to show off the new house as to celebrate his son's good fortune. Patrick didn't get on with his son. He didn't understand him. Patrick didn't understand anything unless it had to do with money but he understood that very well indeed.

He pulled up outside the house in his old Volkswagen Golf and once again felt like the poor relation, parked side by side with flashy BMWs and Mercedes saloons. Now that the business was going well for him Patrick was moving in wealthy circles. For a second he considered reversing out and going home, but then the front door had opened and his sister-in-law was standing in the hallway and he was caught.

'Barry, what kept you?' she called. 'Come on in, every-one else is here!'

Betty was a big, soft sort of a person, kind-hearted and generous but not any kind of a thinker. She saw herself as moving in sophisticated society now, and so she kissed him on the cheek when he arrived. He caught a brief whiff of tobacco and whiskey from her breath. 'How are you, Barry?' she said, pulling him into the light. 'You're looking well. You're losing weight?'

'Trying to.'

'Well, you look terrific. Come in and have a drink.'

'Oh, I'm driving, I can't – '

'Not a bit of it, you'll have a drink and you can stay here tonight if you want, we've plenty of spare rooms.'

'No, really, Betty – '

'Now!' she warned.

The main room was long and L-shaped and full of people, the air swirling with cigarette smoke and throbbing with the background music. There was a loud chatter of conversation, punctuated with bursts of half-suppressed laughter. Patrick came up and pushed a glass of punch into his hand.

'Punch?' he remarked. 'Jesus, Paddy, I remember you and me drinking beer from the bottle!'

His brother roared with laughter. 'Well, we can get on to that later on, if you want,' he said, clapping Barry heavily on back. 'How are you, anyway?'

'I'm great, Paddy, things are good.'

'You look thinner.'

'Well, you're not losing any,' Barry retorted, tapping his brother's protruding gut.

'Took pounds to put that there, Barry, took pounds to put it there.'

More people came up. Brendan pulled his fiancée across and she dutifully showed off the ring and Barry dutifully admired it. She really was a nice little thing, small and dark with smooth green eyes which were very steady. She looked almost indecently young. Brendan stood proudly behind her, his arm around her waist.

'How are you keeping, Brendan?'

'The very best, Uncle Barry. What about this new job

of yours? You'll be inviting us all up for dinner some night, I hope?'

'I only work there, Brendan. I don't own the bloody place.'

'Only a matter of time, though, am I right?'

'You never know, Brendan.'

His other brother Kevin came across, serious as usual. 'Well, Barry,' he said formally. 'How are things with you?'

'All right, Kevin. Can't complain. Who'd listen, anyway?'

'That's true enough.'

Betty came back and took him on a guided tour of the house. There seemed to be hallways and bedrooms everywhere, two bathrooms, one with gold taps, a small bar built into an alcove, a massive kitchen with a big pine table, all with the finest of carpet and floor-coverings. There were people everywhere, most of whom he didn't know. Everyone seemed to be talking about the latest drop in interest rates and how much their mortgage had come down. Betty took him into the kitchen and gave him another glass of punch.

By half-past twelve they had played two rounds of charades and the party had broken up again into small separate groups, people chatting and arguing and laughing with each other. Barry was drunk. He didn't know how it had happened, but all of a sudden his balance had gone and he was having to lean on solid things for support. And his speech was slowing down slightly. Not slurred, because he hated that drunk way of talking, with all your words run into one. Not slurred, but slower and more careful than usual. Mind you, he thought, heaving his way towards the toilet, it's not unpleasant to be drunk. Not in the slightest. Actually, it was quite a nice, light feeling. Not that he would get used to it, or anything, because as a bar manager you had to show a lot of restraint, especially where alcohol was concerned. But it was still nice once in a while. Just now and again.

He got to the toilet and pushed open the door but it was a bedroom with coats laid across the bed. He tried the next door but it was locked. This must be it, he thought. I'll wait for him to finish. Or her, he thought, giggling for no good reason.

There was the sound of the toilet flushing and the scrape of a bolt and the door opened to reveal a vaguely familiar face.

'I know you,' Barry exclaimed.

'You're Barry Kelly,' the other man said, half-smiling. 'I used to work for you. In the River Lodge.'

Barry felt his brain almost whirring, trying to place the face. Tall, spare, dark hair and blue eyes. Then it clicked. Dermot Lavin. One-time barman.

'Yes,' Barry said quickly, pleased to have remembered so fast. 'Dermot Lavin, I remember you. Are you well?'

'I am indeed, and yourself?'

'The very best!' But his brain was working on and suddenly another fact was tossed into his mind. Lavin had been jailed five years before for something or other. Something serious, too. 'Were you not in jail?' Barry asked bluntly.

'I was. I'm out now, though. Changed man.'

He could remember everything else but for the life of

him he couldn't recall what Lavin was supposed to have done.

'Well, it's good to see you again. How come you're here?'

'I know Brendan and Marie from university.'

'You're at university?'

'Aye.'

'Well – look, I'll have to get in here for a pee, or I'll burst.'

'I'll see you later.'

'Right you are.'

Barry stood swaying over the toilet bowl in the quiet of the bathroom, trying to remember what Lavin had done. He remembered him well, a decent lad, worked hard, good timekeeper. What the hell did he do? His mother had phoned in one night to say that he had been arrested and wouldn't be in to work for a while, and about a month after that he heard some more details of the case. He tried to drag it from his memory but the more he dragged the further away it became. Fuck it, he thought suddenly. He went to prison, he's out, he's paid the price. Couldn't have been that serious anyway.

He went out into the main room again to look for Betty, to get somewhere to sleep because his head was spinning. He hated this part of it. His head would spin for a while and it would be like a heavy weight on rails in his head, which slid to and fro every time he moved too quickly. If he didn't get some sleep he would throw up soon.

'Barry!' Brendan and his bride-to-be, apparently still sober, and a tall man with them . . . Lavin, the barman. 'I didn't know you knew Dermot!' Brendan was saying.

'Used to work for me, years ago.'

'God it's a small world, isn't it? Barry's my favourite uncle, Dermot. He's a good guy. Aren't you, Barry?' There was a strong arm suddenly around his shoulders, squeezing.

'We used to have some crack in those days, didn't we?' Lavin was saying. 'Do you remember wee Mickey Murray? And Doherty? And Sheila, do you remember her?'

'Jesus. How could I forget her? She nearly killed me one night!'

'What about that night when the Brits raided the place, and Sheila accused the officer of molesting her? Was that a laugh, or what?'

'I wouldn't have liked to get on her wrong side, even with a whole platoon of soldiers to back me up!'

'Ah, she was a big girl, right enough.'

Brendan and Marie seemed to have drifted off and Barry and Lavin were alone. Barry stepped backwards slightly to lean on the mantelpiece. The fireplace was of massive grey marble. Nice, he thought automatically.

'So what are you doing now, Mr Kelly?'

'It's Barry, Dermot. None of this Mister business, for Christ's sake.'

'Barry.'

'Better.' He told him where he was working.

'Posh,' Lavin commented.

'Not from close up, it's not. It's like everything else in this world, it's deceiving. But it's a good job, I'll say that for it. Nice bar in it.'

Barry felt his stomach begin to slip and slide, and he swallowed to control it. I'm all right, he thought. I'm all right. It's only the drink. He could feel himself swaying away from the fireplace, and he held on firmly.

'I applied for a summer job in there, last year. Long before your time, though. It's a good place to have on your c.v.'

'This is the thing. It's got that name, hasn't it?'

'Did you ever come across a fellow called Mullan? John Mullan? He's a member there?'

'God, yes, I know him well. Talking to him the other day, as a matter of fact. A gentleman, so he is.'

'Aye, he's a nice fellow. I was looking to play a few holes of golf with him sometime.'

'I didn't know you played golf.'

'Just took it up there a few months ago. Very relaxing game.'

'I could never see the sense in it, myself. Never appealed to me.' He hiccuped suddenly. 'Excuse me,' he said, surprised.

'Does he play there a lot?'

'God yes, every Saturday morning, regular as clockwork. He says he wants to get his handicap down.'

'That would be him all right. He's a dedicated sort of a man.'

'That's right. Every bloody Saturday morning, rain or shine. Can't understand it.'

'Well, it isn't everyone's game. But you should have a go at it sometime. Might do you good, to get a feel for the thing. Might help your career.'

Barry laughed. 'The only thing I could do to help my career, Dermot, is change my religion.' The wall seemed to lurch suddenly and the walls began to spin, and he knew with a startling clarity that he was going to be sick. 'I've got to go,' he gasped, pushing past the young man and dashing for the toilet.

In the paper each evening there was a small notice on the top right hand corner, a picture of a hooded man and a number, 'Confidential Telephone, Help Save a Life'. The paper was sitting on the settee in the living room. Colin had memorised the number. The telephone was in the hall. His father was out walking again. All he had to do was lift the phone and dial the number and give the message into the answerphone, that was all, and no one would ever know it was him. It was so easy, and yet so hard. He sat in the silent living room staring at the blank screen of the television and listening as the house creaked and clicked around him. The paper, the phone, his father, they all seemed to be elements of some pattern of force which was squeezing him towards a decision. He could almost imagine flashing lines of energy connecting them all, some unnatural force driving him to the phone, pushing the number into his head, making him speak.

It was three o'clock and he wanted to get out of the house but he would be leaving for work soon anyway and there was no point wandering in the rain. The house was like a cage. He was reminded of lions and tigers pacing in their tiny cages. Everything he went to do seemed to take him past the phone.

The thing was, they had gone too far. It was one thing playing around at being terrorists, but it was another thing entirely to actually get a hold of real guns. That was madness. Sefton was mad, and Hutchy was stupid. The police would catch them and they would go to prison, there was no doubt in Colin's mind about it, and the only question was, how much damage would they do before they were caught? After all, the police wouldn't be actively searching for them. Nobody would know they had the weapons. It was only once they had killed someone, then the police would trace the guns and lean on informants and find out where the things had gone to. And then they would roar around to Sefton's mother's house and drag the madman off to the station, and the same with Hutchy. And with himself?

He went into the hall again and stood looking down at the phone. It seemed to almost glow, as if to pick up the receiver would burn his hand. He could call Piper, and tell him, but Piper was new to the job and he would have to tell them where he got the information from. He could call Mullan. But Mullan had thumped him for nothing. He wouldn't be sympathetic to this.

He picked up the phone and it didn't burn him. He dialled the number for the confidential telephone, slowly, lingering on each digit. They would only get about two or three years, probably, he thought, and

112

remission would cut that down further. And they'd never know who did it. He dialled the last digit, and listened to the bleeps and instructions on the tape, then gently put the receiver down on the cradle again. The palms on his hands were sweating. I don't need this, he was thinking, I don't need this at all.

He wandered back into the living room, then through into the kitchen, then into the living room again. The newspaper was still on the settee. I should sink them for putting me through this bloody agony, he thought. I didn't ask to be involved, they involved me. Bastards.

He heard the sound of a key scraping in the lock and it made him jump. Stevie was back. That's all I need, he thought, cursing inwardly. He sat down on the settee and picked up the paper as the old man hobbled in.

'Hello,' he said gruffly, shrugging off his damp waterproof.

'We're speaking again, are we?' Colin retorted.

'I didn't know we'd stopped. Maybe I missed something.'

'Forget it, then.'

Stevie stood for a moment, staring at him. 'How's your cheek?' he asked.

'I'll live. Your mate Mullan had a go at me, too.'

'Aye, he said.'

'How come you two are so pally?'

'None of your business. Your face is healing up well, anyhow.'

'No thanks to you.'

'It was for your own good.'

'Thanks.'

His father shrugged, and took his coat into the kitchen

113

to hang it up behind the door. I suppose that's as good as an apology as I'm ever going to get, Colin reflected. Stevie came back in and lowered himself into the armchair in front of the television.

'Look,' he began. 'All I was trying to do – '

'I don't want to hear it,' Colin said coolly, beginning to rise.

'You'll hear it, son, now sit back on that settee or I'll break both your fucking legs.'

That dark side of him was flashing again and Colin felt the fear turning over in his chest again. Even with his bad leg he was still a big bastard. He sat down again, slowly.

'That's a bit better. Now. I'm not a great one for words, and I never was. I can't sit down and tell you what's right and what's wrong. I'm pretty sure I know what's right, but maybe I don't know how to say it.' It was all coming out in a bad-tempered rush, and Colin realised that he must have rehearsed the speech many times. 'But I know what's wrong, anyway, because I've done it. You name it, Colin, I've done it. I've broken just about every law there is in my time. And it started just the way it's starting with you. I was hanging around with the wrong people, drinking with the wrong sort of fellows, going to the wrong places.' He rubbed his face with his hand, pinching the bridge of his nose. The veins on the back of his hand were heavy and blue. 'And they got me, Colin, they pulled me in like a fish on a hook. And then, God help me, I pulled other wee lads in, too.' He looked up suddenly, staring up at the wall across the room so intensely that Colin wanted to look too, to see what he was staring at. 'I still have nightmares, son.

I still have the bad dreams. I did things that I'll regret for the rest of my life, and I'll carry them with me to the grave. That's my trouble and it's for me to bear, but Colin, I don't want you to carry the same bloody pain. I don't want it to happen to you. That's all. That's all I want.'

His voice was quivering and Colin was afraid he would cry. 'It's okay,' he said quietly, feeling useless.

They sat silently together for a few minutes as the old man gained control of himself again. 'It's not this leg that makes me the way I am,' Stevie said at last, gesturing at the useless limb. 'This is nothing. It's the memories. The guilt.'

Colin stared across at his father, and it was as though for the first time in his life he truly saw him. The old cardigan with the threadbare elbows. The cheap trousers, cuffs speckled with damp. The lank strands of hair falling forward over his forehead, and the tears glistening in the bloodshot eyes. Suddenly he remembered all the times he had heard the old man sobbing in the locked bathroom, late at night, or the times he had cried himself to sleep on the settee with a bottle of Bush cradled in his lap. They had always thought it was just the pain in his leg making him cry, but maybe it wasn't that, after all. For the first time in his life Colin almost pitied him. What have you carried all these years, he wondered. What the hell did you do?

They sat together in an embarrassed silence for a few minutes longer, then Stevie seemed to gather himself, wiping his forearm across his nose and sniffing loudly. 'Anyway,' he said. 'Is it not about time you were away off to your work?'

'Yes,' said Colin. 'Yes it is. I'd better head over there.'

'Don't be late.'

'No.' He rose uncertainly from the settee. 'I'll . . . see you later, then,' he said.

'Yes. Later on.'

Colin nodded. The old man wasn't looking at him, staring instead at the air in front of his face. He looked old. Old and beaten. Colin slipped out of the room and pulled the door gently behind him.

The golf club was busy. It was bingo night and there were a lot of guests in and Ernie and Colin were running the bar on their own again, working smoothly together now, dodging around each other on their way to the till. Barry Kelly had a headache and stayed in his office most of the evening, only emerging to fetch himself mugs of strong black coffee from the kitchen.

By the end of the night the ashtrays were full and the tables were covered in empty glasses, and only one table of die-hards was left in the corner, laughing and singing and heckling each other. Colin picked his way around them, collecting the empties. Mullan was in the group, not as drunk as the rest, but red-faced and happy looking. He hadn't once looked towards Colin all evening. Colin wrinkled his eyes and felt the remnants of the bruise thick and tender on his cheek. Bastard.

'What do you think of Mullan, Ernie?' he asked.

'Oh, he's all right. Tips well, now and again.'

'Have you ever got on his wrong side?'

Ernie shook his head. 'No. Wouldn't care to, either. I'd say he could be a right hard fellow, if he wanted to.'

116

He looked up quickly, grinning. 'But then, you'd already know that, wouldn't you?'

Mullan's group were beginning to get up, the women gathering up their handbags and the men draining the last of their pints. Colin waited until the first few had drifted away from the table before going out to collect the empty glasses. He wrinkled his nose at the state of the table, strewn with glasses and bottles and empty cigarette packets, the ashtray overflowing.

'Colin.'

He straightened up slowly, two empty pint glasses clamped in his fingers. It was Mullan, standing slightly off to one side, smiling slightly.

'Mr Mullan,' Colin acknowledged him stiffly.

'I wanted to apologise about the other night. I should never have done that. I'm sorry.' He stuck out his big hand. 'No hard feelings?'

Colin looked from his face to his hand and back to his face again, confused, not sure what to do. Eventually he set down the pint glasses and took the offered hand.

'Okay,' he said, sensing the big policeman's strength.

'Good.' Mullan let go of his hand and made to turn away and Colin suddenly realised that this would be a good time to say something, to drop a hint, even, anything that Mullan could follow up.

'Mr Mullan,' he said. Mullan paused.

'Yes?'

'Ah . . . you were right, about Sefton and Hutchy . . . I mean . . . they're not a good influence . . . I'm not going to . . .' A word flashed into his head in great, neon letters; INFORMER, it read, INFORMER. Tout. Grass. He had a sudden image of Hutchy in a prison cell for the next ten years, his big, stupid head hanging down, his eyes heavy. Colin felt his conscience shy away. 'Can I ask you something?' he said.

'If it's quick, yes. Go ahead.'

'What was it that Stevie did?'

He watched Mullan's face for a reaction but there was nothing, just a slight, barely noticeable relaxing of the mouth into the beginnings of a smile. He reached out and clapped a big hand on to Colin's shoulder.

'You once accused me of interfering with your family too much. And you were right. Colin, it's up to your father to tell you that; I can't tell you for him. I know you don't talk to each other all that much, but he's the man that'll have to tell you. But I tell you what. You shouldn't have such a low opinion of him. Talk to him.' He smiled broadly. There were three or four people waiting for him at the door. 'I've got to go now. See you again, Colin.'

Colin nodded. 'Thanks,' he said. Then Mullan had slipped through the door and suddenly the lounge was still and empty, except for the debris of the drinking and the stink of cigarettes and spilled beer.

For a week Colin lived in a half-light of frightened anticipation, always expecting to hear the ring of the door-bell and to see the visor of an RUC cap gleaming through the oval frosted window, deep voices asking if Colin was in and could he come down to the station with them. Every night, when he came back from the golf club and fell exhausted into bed, he lay for hours staring at the ceiling, running over the options and chances in his mind. He was more frightened than he had ever been in his life. Sefton had obtained those weapons to use on people, and that would mean murder. Death. There was no doubt in Colin's mind that someone was going to die, and that if he did nothing their deaths would weigh just as much on his conscience as if he had pulled the trigger himself. It was too serious. And yet he did nothing, said nothing. All it would take would be a phone call. Every night the number of the confidential telephone seemed to burn deeper into his mind, until he thought that no matter how old he came to be there would still be sleepless nights when the bloody thing would still glow faintly in his head.

The more he considered it, the more Mullan came to mind as a likely way out. Their last meeting had been kindly enough, they had made up and were friends again. Mullan would perhaps give him advice. But if he disclosed enough information to Mullan to enable him to advise, then he would get the rest out of him, somehow or other. So he might as well just tell the policeman the lot, and have done with it. But then he would be involved, too, as an accomplice. The whole thing just went round and round; there was no way of letting the police know without becoming involved himself.

He had visions and dreams, of courtrooms, trials, inquests. Sobbing families listening as the last moments of their loved ones were read out. The accusing finger pointed at himself. I could have prevented it, my Lord, but I said nothing. I am guilty. He woke up in the fuzzy darkness of the bedroom with the indistinct shapes of furniture looming at him, sweat sticking the sheets to his skin, his throat dry.

By the middle of the week he had resolved to come clean and tell Mullan the whole story. There was no other way. He could fiddle the dates a little to make it seem that he had only just found out, and had gone straight to the policeman, and he really hadn't done anything wrong. He hadn't handled the guns. He didn't help to hide them. His only crime was knowing, and doing nothing. He would tell Mullan and Mullan would understand. And then he could relax a little.

Colin worked on Wednesday and Thursday on the

120

late shift but Mullan didn't appear. He thought about phoning him at the police station but somehow it would be easier to explain face-to-face, where he could see how the policeman was taking it. He wasn't due to work on Friday night, but on Thursday he carefully left a sports bag behind, so that he could call for it on Friday. Mullan wasn't there on Friday, either.

On Saturday he was due to work from four to eleven but he swapped a shift with another barman in order to get the morning, eleven to six. Mullan always played golf on Saturday mornings, and Colin reckoned he could probably catch him just before he left the club at lunchtime.

It was a clear, bright winter day, and outside all the noises from the yard seemed to clatter in the still air. Golfers were standing round, fiddling with their bags and trolleys, their studs clicking on the cold cobbles. Colin wheeled a few crates of Coke and white lemonade from the store across the yard, and all the bottles rattled and crashed as the old trolley bounced on the uneven surface. The sun glinted on puddles. The air was clean. In the main lounge the sunlight was slanting in through the big windows and reflecting on the glasses and bottles arrayed on the shelves behind the bar, making broad strips of light across the soft velour upholstery. There was no one about and the lounge was empty. At half eleven Barry Kelly wandered in and flicked his head towards the empty room.

'What the hell have you done to all the customers, Colin?' he asked jokingly.

'They're all hid behind the curtains, there, Mr Kelly,' Colin replied. 'Heard you were coming.'

'Very good,' he said cheerfully. 'I like a man with a sense of humour. Hope you're as smart in your exams.' He came in behind the bar and leaned on the counter, staring out through the sunlit windows and grinning cheerfully. 'It's nice here on a day like this,' he remarked easily. 'Very relaxing. I can see why people would become members here.'

'You wouldn't happen to know if Mr Mullan is playing today, would you?' Colin asked.

'Yeah, he was in earlier on, as a matter of fact, leaving in his fees. Why?'

'Oh, nothing much. I've got a message for him from my da.'

'I see.' Barry chewed at his lip for a moment. 'Look, it's none of my business, but I couldn't help noticing the wee bit of trouble you had there, last week. I didn't want to say anything in front of the other staff. But if you're having trouble, and you think I could help, you know, just give me a shout.'

'Thanks. But there's no trouble.'

'You're sure?'

Colin nodded. 'I probably deserved what I got.'

Barry seemed satisfied. 'Right, then,' he said. 'I'm nipping across to the professional's shop. See you later on.'

'Okedoke, Mr Kelly.'

An old couple came in and took their half pints of lager by the window, gazing quietly out at the blue sky and the grey trees. Colin changed a couple of kegs, and restocked the shelves with Diet Coke and splits. He switched on the radio behind the bar and listened to Radio One for a while, keeping the volume down as

122

low as he could. After a while Barry Kelly came back in, rubbing his hands from the cold.

'Mullan's out there now, in the car park,' he said. 'If you want to go and talk to him, I'll mind the bar for a while.'

'Oh, right. Thanks, Mr Kelly.'

Colin walked nervously out into the crisp air, still unsure of what exactly he should say. The chill gripped him hard through his thin white shirt. He would just tell the whole story, he decided, as quickly as he could, and end up with the guns at Sefton's house. They were bound to be there; Sefton would have them close enough to play with. The police would find them hidden somewhere in the house.

Mullan was at the far side of the car park, standing by the open hatch of his Sierra and stuffing something into a pocket of his golf bag. He was wearing a canary yellow pullover and a tweed flat cap. Colin felt his mouth dry up as he approached. It was the way he felt on the way to the dentist, frightened and wary but trapped by circumstance.

There was another man walking towards the policeman, probably one of his group, and Colin wondered if he should hold off until he got Mullan alone. He paused behind a parked car, and watched as the other man walked up to Mullan and spoke briefly to him. Mullan straightened up, and the other man pulled something from inside his jacket and pointed it straight out towards Mullan's head and then Colin heard the shots, three shots, one after the other, each one jolting the policeman's head with the impact. Jesus Christ, Colin thought, they're shooting Mullan. Mullan staggered slightly, then fell slowly against the open back of his car and slid down until his head was leaning against the bumper. The gunman leaned forward and pointed the gun right at Mullan's forehead, moving with a terrible ease, then first another shot. Colin wanted to look away. I don't want to see this, he thought frantically. Mullan fell over onto the tarmac, his hat falling on the ground beside him. The gunman put the gun calmly back inside his jacket and walked quickly away, gaining speed as he went until by the time he reached the treeline he was sprinting. Colin stood frozen. Mullan was twenty feet from him. His mind was still ringing from the deafening banging of the gun. What do I do, he thought, what do I do? He moved forward, unsteadily, banging his shin on a car bumper. He felt sick. Mullan was lying on his side, a spout of blood spraying upwards from his head and falling into his flat cap, filling it up. Other people were rushing towards him, nudging Colin roughly aside, kneeling by him, shouting, putting their hands across the dreadful wounds. No use, Colin thought, he's dead. He was dead after the first shot. He's dead. Someone was shouting, cursing and weeping. There was a small crowd around the body now, kneeling down by his head. Colin could no longer see the wound, but he glanced up at the open hatchback of the Sierra and saw that the inside of the rear window had been soiled with blood and other things. Then his stomach heaved at last and he bent over and threw up on the tarmac.

Barry heard the first three shots from the lounge and for a second he tried unsuccessfully to convince himself that they might be something else, a car backfiring perhaps, or someone hammering, not necessarily a murder. Then he heard the final shot and it was unmistakable and his stomach fell away.

He hurried out into the car park and saw the commotion around the open hatchback and he ran up to see what had happened. There were people kneeling around a body on the ground. Someone was shouting about an ambulance. Barry wanted to see who it was, he had to see who it was. He felt empty in his stomach, frightened, afraid to look. He grasped someone by the arm.

'What happened?' he asked urgently. 'Who is it?'

'John Mullan. He's been shot.'

'Is he dead?'

'I don't know.'

He moved forward to the edge of the commotion and

suddenly someone stood up and darted away, giving him a clear view of the shattered head and the thick pool of blood now overflowing the cap. Oh Jesus Mary and Joseph, he thought, involuntarily crossing himself. Someone caught the quick movement and stared angrily at him. To hell with you, Barry thought.

The police arrived shortly after that, screaming into the car-park in an armoured Sierra, leaping out and shooing people away from the body. When they saw the extent of the injuries their urgency lessened a little. Two of them began to close off the scene with rolls of white tape. More vehicles arrived; another car, two grey Land-rovers, an ambulance. One of the policemen sat in the front of a car with his head in his hands and his shoulders heaving and jerking. Radios crackled and hissed.

Barry went back into the clubhouse, a little unsteady on his feet. Fifteen years before he had seen a young soldier shot dead in Derry and now it all came back to him, every last detail recorded in his memory as a dreadful souvenir. The boy rolling about on the pavement, screaming, as his colleagues tried to stop the pumping flow of blood. His fingers, reaching out and grasping for something just at the moment he died. The people standing about, curiously embarrassed as though having witnessed something personal and intimate. Some of the other soldiers had stepped in the growing pool of his blood and their boots had left prints on the dry grey pavement, scarlet bloody footprints; the image had seared itself into his brain. Twice, he thought, I've had to suffer this twice. Well, thank you Jesus, I hope you had a good reason.

126

There were some women weeping in the hallway, and he eased his way around them, trying not to listen. He found Colin behind the bar in the lounge, sitting on an upturned plastic crate, his face ashen.

'Help me shut the bar, Colin,' he said.

The boy nodded, and began to pull down the shutters. The familiar scraping, rolling clunk which had always seemed so welcome before sounded distant and alien now.

'Mr Mullan has been shot,' Barry said distantly.

'I know,' Colin replied. 'I saw it happen. He's dead.'

'You saw it? What happened?'

'A fellow came up to him and shot him. Just . . . shot him.'

'Look, you'd better come out with me, and tell the police what you saw. They'll need as much information as they can get.' Barry felt better now, there was something to do, something useful. He locked the bar up, then steered Colin by the shoulders out to the car park.

That night Angie sat with Colin in the quiet kitchen holding his hand, still in her coat, both of them leaning slightly forward over the formica table-top. She watched him carefully, her eyes damp and concerned. Stevie stalked up and down the length of the worktop, the rubber tip of his walking stick thudding on the lino.

'What did they ask you, love?' she asked gently.

'They asked me about the gunman. What he was like. They wanted to know what he was wearing.'

'And did you tell them?'

'Yes.'

He felt like a ten-year-old, but the words would not

come, and he needed her to coax them from him. His mind was numb. Nothing seemed to work the way it used to. He was trying to stop the picture replaying itself again and again in his head, the cloth cap filling with the thick, dark blood, the shattered head, the steam rising from it. It was on a loop, again and again and again.

'Did you see where he went to, love?'

'Who?'

'The gunman.'

'He ran towards the trees. I mean, he walked at first, then he got faster. He was running when he got to the trees.'

'Bastards!' Stevie spat from behind him. The electric clock on the wall clicked loudly in the silence. Angie looked briefly up at her husband, admonishing him.

'They want me to come down to the station tomorrow,' Colin said.

'What for?'

'They need me to make another statement. And I think they want me to look at photographs.'

'You'll need to let your boss know – '

'He's got to do down, too.'

The detective had been very interested in Barry Kelly. They had taken him into his office and spoken to him for more than two hours, which was half an hour longer than Colin's longest stretch. And he had still been at the police station when they let Colin go home, so God only knew when he was getting out. It was a pity because he was a good man. He had been steady just when Colin needed something to grasp at.

128

'That's that fellow from the Bogside, is it?' Stevie snorted.

'He's all right,' Colin protested.

'Aye,' Stevie said, not believing.

'How do you feel, love?' his mother asked.

'I'm all right. I was sick earlier on.'

'I'm sure you were. Do you want to go on up to bed, and I'll make you up a good hot water bottle?'

'No, no, I'm all right.'

'Are you sure you wouldn't like to? A wee bit of sleep might do you good.' She had reached out and was stroking the hair away from his forehead and he felt like a child again but there was no chance of sleep with this thing in his head. Not for a long time yet. Over and over again, the last shot, right into the forehead. Dear God.

His mother half-rose and went to put her arm around him and he recoiled instinctively, moving away slightly.

'No, Mum, honestly!'

He had snapped at her and her face showed the hurt. She subsided into her seat again, chewing her lower lip. The clock ticked. I'm sorry Mum, he was thinking, then suddenly and without warning he was crying, weeping, his lip twisting like a baby's, hating himself for his weakness. Angie went quickly around to him and tried to hug him but he wrenched free and the betrayal hurt him all the more.

'Colin – '

'Leave him to me,' Stevie was saying, shrugging on his walking coat. 'Get him his coat.' His voice was flat, commanding.

'You're not taking him anywhere! The child's exhausted, can you not see that?'

'He's not a child.'

'Well, he's not much more! He should be in bed and asleep – '

'Ah, for God's sake, woman!' Stevie roared suddenly. 'He's just seen a man murdered! Do you think he'll sleep after that?' He stood awkwardly, leaning on his stick with Colin's jacket in one hand, glaring at his wife. After a few seconds he tossed the jacket at Colin. 'Come on,' he said.

They walked westwards towards the strand, the cold breeze ruffling their hair and watering their eyes, their hands deep in their pockets. Neither of them spoke for some time. They turned off the road and down on to the path which led to the beach, away from the street-lights and into the smell of salt and seaweed. At last Colin broke the silence.

'Mum will be crying.'

'She'd be crying anyway, even if you were up in bed.'

'Aye.'

The path wound down the side of a hotel and they cut across the floodlit car park, small and naked in the bright expanse of empty tarmac. The smell of the sea was stronger now, the noise of the waves rushing in from the darkness. Beyond the floodlights the sea had its own luminescence, gradually becoming clearer as their eyes adjusted to the dark.

The path led to the steps, and the steps led down to the strand, three miles of gently curving beach, with the sea on one side and the dunes on the other. The dunes were a magical mystery world where a boy could lose himself for a whole day and never cross the same hill twice. Colin had spent a lot of time in there as a kid, rolling around in the stiff beach grass. At night a few cars would drive on to the beach and park facing the sea, their lights out, looking like collapsed beetles on a pale carpet, but they never went very far from the entrance. If you bogged down at night there was no one to help you out.

'It's nice here at night,' Stevie said, as they walked down on to the sand.

'Is this where you walk?'

'Aye. Most times.'

It was cold and sharp and the wind buffeted his ears but it was clean, gloriously clean. In the distance they could see a string of lights on the Donegal coast. It was hard to believe that anyone could commit murder in a place as peaceful as this.

'You have to get out of the house, Colin, in times like this,' Stevie said. 'All the women want to do is weep and wail, and that'll only get you down. Out of the house. Women love a tragedy, so they do. They live on it. Look at the way your ma goes through those bloody death notices in the paper.'

Colin smiled thinly. True enough, he thought.

'You're better out of it.'

They walked in silence past the parked cars. Lucky people, Colin thought bitterly, they weren't tangled up in murder. They hadn't seen a man killed for nothing. It was just unfair. Mullan was a good man and they killed him, when there were hundreds of bastards about, ripe for the taking.

'How did you know Mullan?' he asked.

'He, ah, he came out to check on me when we first moved up here. They were worried about me then. Didn't know what sort of state I was in. They needn't have bothered. Anyway, he came out to the house and we had a chat.'

'He called quite a bit, didn't he? In the beginning.'

'Aye, well I was able to do him a few favours, you know.' There was a tone in his voice which said, no further, and Colin didn't press it. He wiped at his face with his sleeve.

'I never would have believed there was so much blood in a man,' he said quietly. His father nodded slowly.

'You'd think it would never stop,' he agreed. 'I got my first sight of blood in a butcher's yard, you know. Your Uncle Bobby used to work in McCammon's butchers on the Shankill, and I used to go round there now and again for messages. I was about nine, this day, and he took me round the back and they were slaughtering this calf. God knows where they got it from, but they had killed it and they were just hanging it up when I arrived. The blood that poured out of that thing! I thought it was never going to stop! Jesus, you should have seen the state of me bouncing around there, frightened out of my wits, with all this blood landing on the floor around me.' He laughed shortly at the memory, and Colin laughed too. 'Thing is, Colin, we're only animals, really. You, me, Mullan. That's all we are. We just get ideas above our station. But someday we'll all end up rotting in the ground, just like any other cow or horse or pig.'

'I never saw anyone die before.'

'You'll get used to it. You'll never forget it, but you'll get used to it, and you'll tuck it somewhere in the back of your head and it'll only come out in nightmares. But at least you've seen it. You've nothing more to be scared of now. There's nothing much worse than that.'

They walked for an hour, almost to the end of the beach then back again, now and again talking quietly to each other. Next morning Colin couldn't remember much of what he had said, but he remembered the long silences with only the rushing sound of the surf and the buffeting of the wind in his ears and the new feeling of discomfort. By the time they made it back to the house, there were no lights on downstairs.

'Your ma's away to bed in a huff,' Stevie said quietly, looking up at the bedroom window.

'I think I'd better get some sleep, too,' Colin said.

'You'd better try, I suppose.'

Stevie kicked his shoes on the doorstep to knock off the loose sand, then pushed the key into the door.

'Thanks for the walk, dad,' Colin said.

'No problem,' Stevie said quickly, lumbering quickly into the darkened hallway.

There was a barely visible scrawl in spidery blue biro on the plain white wall facing him across the interview room. 'Fucking RUC bastards', it said. It was the only reminder of humanity in the entire room; the bare table, the plain, naked walls, even the battered tin ashtray could all have been produced by a monstrous regime of robots but it was a human who had scrawled that scratch of anger. Barry sat at the bare table and felt the walls closing in around him. His stomach was churning from the nervous tension, and he couldn't keep his hands still, tapping them on the worn formica top or fiddling with the ashtray, keeping them busy so they wouldn't just tremble.

He was frightened because they wouldn't let him go home, always saying they had just a few more questions for him. In the back of his mind he had a notion that they couldn't really keep him there, but they were tall men with guns and he didn't want to annoy them. They were annoyed enough as it was. Maybe I should ask for a lawyer, he thought, maybe I'm entitled to one, or was that just in America. It seemed like he knew more about American law, from the TV, than he did about the law in his own country. On TV you were always entitled to one phone call. But then they hadn't charged him with anything, all he was doing was helping their enquiries.

They suspected him of being involved in the murder. He understood that and it did not make him angry, because after all he came from the Bogside and there were a lot of people there who were involved in things. People made these assumptions and it was natural. But there was a little anger in him all the same, glowing deep down inside and flaring every time he turned his mind towards it, because to them he was nothing but another Fenian bastard. All his work, all his skills, all that time and energy spent dragging himself out of the gutter and in the final analysis he might never have bothered. Just another Fenian bastard.

He checked his watch again and it was almost seven o'clock, nearly five hours since they had asked him to come down to the station. They would surely let him go home soon. It wasn't as if he had even seen anything, and even if he had they wouldn't have had to ask for it.

At ten past seven the tall detective came in. Barry had forgotten his name. He was tall and slim with thick wavy fair hair and a long scar behind his right ear. Barry pulled himself upright in the chair and leaned forward across the table, watching him carefully as he pulled out the chair and sat down opposite him. He was carrying a sheaf of papers which he set down on the table-top.

'Just a few more questions for you, Mr Kelly,' he said

evenly. He had been consistently polite but his eyes betrayed him; I hate you, they said, you murdered my friend and I hate you for it.

'Is this going to take much longer?' Barry asked.

'There's a man lying in the morgue tonight who was a friend of mine this morning, Mr Kelly,' the policeman said in a flat and expressionless voice. 'We'll get you home tonight at some point in time. He isn't going home ever again.'

'Yes, I know, I'm sorry, look . . . I'm sorry.' Barry clasped his hands on the table and stared down at them, feeling ashamed and ridiculous. He was suddenly embarrassed by the length of his fingernails and he slipped his hands on to his lap.

'I'm going to read out a few names here,' the policeman went on. 'What I want you to do is tell me if you know any of them, or have heard of them. All right?'

'Yes.'

'Okay.' He picked up a sheet of paper and began to read the names out in a slow, resonant voice, pausing briefly after each name, his eyes flickering up to watch for any reaction. Barry was suddenly reminded of his old class teacher at St Mary's, sonorously calling out the morning roll without listening for the answers.

'Kevin Graham. Sean Allison. Michael McCoy. James Bartlett. Patrick McDonagh.' At each name Barry shook his head. 'Gerry Lynch. Brian Doherty.'

'There was a Brian Doherty used to work for a garage where I got my car serviced. I didn't know him well. A mechanic.'

'No, this one's no mechanic.' Pause. 'Peter Convery.' Pause. 'Dermot Lavin.'

Barry felt his body stiffen involuntarily and suddenly it was all clear to him, like a tightened knot which had suddenly fallen open, all horribly simple and open and clear. Lavin had been in the IRA and that was why he had gone to prison and he should have realised, he should have remembered. He had been involved in a bombing of some sort. He had been in it up to his neck, and those people never change their spots. That was why he had been interested in Mullan, they were never going to play golf together, Lavin was up to his neck in it and Barry had helped to set it up. He felt his head getting light. His stomach turned over. Dear God, he thought, what have I done?

The detective had noticed his flicker of panic and was watching him, waiting. Jesus Christ, Barry thought, feeling the panic surging through his system, I'm right into it now. What do I do? His head reeled. He had to say something and the sensible thing would be to let them have everything, every detail, get it all out into the open as soon as possible because if they thought he was hiding something then he was finished. And if Lavin had been involved in the murder then Barry owed him no favours. But an older, deeper part of him was comparing Lavin and the policeman and it was saying, it's them and us, and Lavin is one of us. He took a slow breath, trying to calm himself.

'I know him,' he said hesitantly. 'He used to work in a bar I managed.'

'When did you last see him?'

The thing was that maybe they knew Lavin had been at the party, you never could tell what they knew, and if they knew that then this question was a test. But if

Barry turned Lavin in, the rest of them would come looking for him. Informer. Life wouldn't be worth living. Then he thought of Mullan lying on the tarmac and his shattered, steaming head and he thought, well, at least you'd have a life to live. 'He was at a party. At my brother's house.' He gave the address.

'When?'

'Last Friday night.'

'You were speaking to him?'

'Yes, just for a bit. Just said hello.'

'What did he say to you?'

Barry tried to think of something to say. He didn't want to inform on Lavin. God will judge him, he thought desperately, it isn't up to us. Vengeance is the Lord's. It was clear to him now that Lavin had been asking about Mullan with a view to passing the information on, and he had told him exactly where and when to find him. If he hadn't opened his big mouth Mullan might still be alive. 'We talked about my nephew; it was his engagement party. Lavin said he was at Queen's with my nephew. We talked a bit about the golf club.' He was getting close to the dangerous bit and his palms were sweating.

'Did he ask you about the club?'

'Yes, he did. About the bar, that sort of thing. He used to work in bars. He was interested.'

'Did he mention Mr Mullan at all?'

Here it comes here it comes, dear God help me.

'No.'

Pause. Barry felt his pulse begin to race, hammering in his chest. He knows, he thought, he knows I'm lying. And why am I lying? Because I helped to kill that man and I don't want to go to prison. You deserve to go to prison. But I didn't know. That's no excuse.

'Did he mention where he'd been over the past few years?'

'I knew he'd been in jail. I asked him when he'd got out.'

'How do you feel about your family mixing with people like that?'

'Well . . . he went to prison. He did his time. You've got to give him a chance.'

'There's a good chance that your friend Lavin is involved in this murder.'

'I . . . I wouldn't have thought it.'

'Well, you'd better believe it. And if he didn't pull the trigger, then he's bloody close to the man who did.' The detective was leaning forward now, across the table, his hands clasped in front of his chest. 'You meet him at a party, and a week later he murders a policeman in your golf club. That's a bit of a coincidence, isn't it?'

'Well, I don't know – '

'And with your background, and everything. A man could be excused for supposing that you fingered Mullan.'

'I happened to like Mr Mullan, actually.'

'Didn't stop you setting him up.'

'I didn't set him up.'

'Would have been very easy, though, wouldn't it?'

'I DIDN'T SET HIM UP!' Barry shouted suddenly, feeling a sudden overpowering urge to weep, waves of guilt and fear and anger washing through him in turn. 'I didn't set him up! I didn't do anything! I heard the shots, I offered to help, then you keep me in here for hours on end and accuse me of all sorts of things! For God's sake, I didn't do anything!'

The detective eased his chair back and slowly placed his palms behind his head, screwing up his eyes and relaxing them again. The room was silent. From somewhere outside came the faint sound of a car horn. The policeman was poised and confident in his neat clothes and his expensive slip-on shoes, and Barry was painfully aware of how ridiculous he must look; overweight, middle-aged, untidy, his face red and his jacket rumpled. With a great wave of depression he felt terribly sorry for himself.

'Ever since I mentioned Lavin's name you've been shitting yourself, haven't you?' the detective said at last.

'No.'

'Your face went white. Your forehead is sweating.' He suddenly uncoiled himself and lunged over towards Barry, reaching out and seizing his wrist. His grip was very strong. He shook at the wrist to open up the hand. 'Look at those palms,' he snapped, 'They're soaking. I wouldn't be surprised if you've wet yourself as well.' He released the wrist and subsided back down into his chair. Barry rubbed at the reddened skin, feeling helpless and near to tears.

'I was frightened,' he said.

'Of what?'

'Once you found out I knew Lavin you'd assume I was involved.'

'I think you're involved anyway.'

'You're wrong.'

'I'm not wrong, Mr Kelly. I've been in this business too bloody long. I can spot a liar a mile off. And you,

Mr Kelly, are lying. I have no doubt of it. You and I both know that you are lying. The only thing is, can I prove it?'

'I'm not lying, honestly,' Barry pleaded.

'Well, if you aren't, then I won't be able to prove anything, will I?'

Barry was about to retort but he controlled himself, turning his gaze down towards his lap. They sat in silence for a moment.

'Well,' said the detective. 'I suppose there isn't much more I can get out of you at the moment.' Barry let all the air of his lung in a long sigh of relief. 'But listen,' the detective said quietly. 'I'm going to be watching you. If I think you're so much as trying to fart in the wrong place, I'll lift you and we'll do this all over again. Am I making this clear enough to you?'

'Yes,' Barry said. 'Don't worry.'

'Good.' He unclasped his arms and rubbed vigourously at his eyes. 'Well, Mr Kelly,' he said heavily. 'Thanks very much for your help. I'll get one of the boys to run you home. I've got to try to think of something to say to a grieving widow tonight.'

The police car stopped at the gates of the club and Barry got out into the chilly night air. His breath swirled around his head. 'Thanks,' he said back into the car. The two policemen said nothing. The engine was still running and it seemed very loud in the stillness. Oh, for God's sake, Barry thought. He slammed the door hard and stepped back as the police car pulled off into the road and disappeared into the darkness. 'Fuck you!' Barry said sharply to the surrounding shadows.

He set off to walk the quarter of a mile from the gates to the clubhouse. There were tall trees on each side of the drive and their bare branches rustled and rattled above him as he walked, and all the way to the clubhouse he had the feeling that there was someone watching him from the shadows. He tried not to let his footsteps ring on the frosty tarmac.

The thing was that he had helped to get a man murdered. That was the long and the short of it, the bottom line. Mullan was dead and he wouldn't be dead if he, Barry, hadn't got drunk and talked his head off. Of course, they would have probably got the information from someone else, or they would have killed him somewhere else, but that wasn't the point. It had happened here, it had happened to him, and it was his bloody fault.

The police would find that out if they ever picked up Lavin. He would tell them where he got the information from; why shouldn't he? And that would be the end of it all; no more job, no more managing, no more cash. Prison, maybe. And when he got out, who was going to employ an old ex-con who used to be a bar manager? Hopelessness swilled around in his gut. He was caught in a trap and there was no way out of it.

The clubhouse loomed up out of the darkness, squat and brooding and still and there was something odd about it which he couldn't work out and then he realised that all the lights were off, save on over the front door. He had never seen the clubhouse with all the lights off before. There had always been lights on.

He walked quickly past the empty car park and forced himself not to look towards it, half afraid of what he might see. What would you do, he thought, if you turned around and saw Mullan standing there with half his head blown off, over there, in the shadows beneath the trees. Watching. He felt his spine shudder, then chided himself for his imagination. The man is dead. Finish.

He let himself in by the side door, his eyes fixed on the key and the lock, not looking into the shadows on either side. Don't be a fool, he told himself. Calm

143

down. The hall light was on and a tiny line of yellow light showed at the top of the door. His fingers were cold and he fumbled with the key and suddenly, out of nothing, there came a dreadful, compelling need to get inside and away from the clutching darkness. There were awful things lumbering at him and he had to get away. Panic rattled in his chest and he pushed and heaved at the key and then the door opened and he fell through and slammed it quickly shut behind him.

He stood against the door for a long time, trying to gather his wits about him, trying to calm himself. I'm cracking up, he thought. I'm going round the bend. The hallway was empty and the silence of the empty clubhouse rang in his ears, and a muscle in his thigh was twitching uncontrollably. I can't stay here tonight, I couldn't sleep here. There is madness here.

He let the minutes slide past in the whining silence, fighting down a rushing urge to weep. It isn't my fault, he thought, rubbing at his eyes. I didn't do anything. He squeezed his eyelids tight and felt the water trickle down his cheeks and it became somehow very important to him not to let go, not to dissolve into a flood of childish tears. He sniffed. He had the keys of the bar in his pocket. He could have a drink or two before bed. Just to settle the stomach. And the mind.

He stood for a few moments more and listened to the silence and then his mind was suddenly made up and he pushed off the door and, jangling the bunch of keys in his pocket, he went off to get as pole-axed as he could.

The machine-gun juddered in his hands and he was doing very well for a change, hitting everything in sight, wiping them out as fast as they came for him. A soldier burst out from a doorway and Colin switched fire and watched the impact knock him over, switching again to a helicopter which had swung to a hover over the buildings. He pressed the button for the grenade launcher and the chopper exploded and disappeared.

'You're doing well,' Hutchy said casually.

'Aye,' Colin said breathlessly. There were hand grenades and knives coming at him from all directions now and his ammunition was perilously low and then it was finished and the screen was flashing 'Game Over' at him, urging him to put in some more coins.

'Put more money in,' Hutchy said, his mouth full of crisps. 'That's a good score. Don't waste it.'

'Fuck it,' Colin said casually. He had used the last of his ten-pence pieces and the cash was all gone.

'I'll do it, then,' Hutchy said, pushing past him and slotting a coin into the machine. The plastic Uzi looked petite in his big hands.

It was the best game in the arcade. Better than the space invaders or the old pinball machines. You could feel the gun shaking in your hand and you could see your bullets kicking up the dirt on the screen, and when you hit the enemy they fell over dead. A good game.

Hutchy started his game, firing at everything, holding the trigger constantly open and spraying anything that moved on the screen. The old version of the game used to have hostages who appeared at the windows but Hutchy had just wasted them, too. No finesse.

Colin looked around the arcade for a familiar face but there were only five people in the place and they were mostly kids. A girl in skin-tight jeans stood talking to a fellow who was playing the poker game. He was sitting on a tall stool, smoking a hand-rolled cigarette, ignoring her. She had long fairish hair tied back into a pony-tail. Colin had seen her around town but he didn't know her. He thought the arcade was a depressing place. It was dark and tatty and seedy, and people only went there when they had nothing better to do. It was better in the summer, when the trippers were up and there was sunlight through the glass doors at the far end, but even then there would be boys up from Belfast or Derry who would cause aggro just for the sake of it.

'Bugger!' Hutchy spat under his breath, his eyes fixed on the screen. He would never beat Colin's score. He wasted all his ammo and grenades, when what was called for was precision shooting, making every bullet count. Hutchy had never got past the fourth level, and it annoyed him. Finally he was finished and the machine beeped and sang at him. He slapped disgustedly at the machine-gun. 'Stupid fucking game, anyway,' he said.

They walked up the promenade towards the harbour, heading for the newsagent so that Hutchy could buy some fags. Colin had the hood of his anorak pulled up around his head and the rain pitter-pattered lightly on the thin blue nylon.

'Sefton wanted to know if you were all right, by the way,' Hutchy said casually.

'Why shouldn't I be?'

'After seeing your man getting wasted. He thought you might have been upset.'

'I'm all right.'

'That's what I told him. I told him you'd be all right. He's strange sometimes, so he is.'

'That's an understatement.'

They were walking along the promenade and the rain was drifting in from the sea and the waves were washing gently on to the rocks and nothing had changed, not a thing. Then why did it all feel so different? The town, the harbour, the arcade, everything seemed somehow pointless and unreal, now that he knew how life could so suddenly end. It was as if you had spent your entire life walking round blindfold, until someone suddenly whipped the thing away and you realised you were standing in the middle of a minefield. Death had never really intruded into his life before; he was too young to appreciate the inevitable slowing down and ending of existence. On the television, yes, on the news reports, in the papers. In films and videos. Death was around, it was out there, clean, sanitised death which was too far away to matter, which the cameras didn't linger on. Now there was death. It had become fact. It had a reality in his memory. Now he knew that there was nothing inside a man's head but pulpy grey and red stuff.

Hutchy bought his cigarettes and there was nothing else to do so they walked up the hill towards Sefton's house. At least I can fiddle with his guitar, Colin thought morosely.

'What about the guns, Hutchy?' he asked.

'Sefton has them hid. I haven't seen them.'

'What's he going to do with them?'

'Fuck knows. Wank over them, probably.'

Sefton still had the guns and Hutchy was still involved with him and it was all still illegal but what did it matter now? Laws had assumed a lesser importance, like weeds around a statue. There were more important things in life than laws. Mullan's life had ebbed away on to the dirty rain-washed tarmac and none of the laws on earth had prevented it or could change it. So Sefton had guns. So what?

Sefton saw them coming up the path and was waiting at the door for them. He was wearing brown felt carpet slippers over his dark blue patterned socks, and an Aran cardigan in a strange shade of cream. He kept his face long and solemn as they approached. 'Come in, boys,' he said with gravity. 'Come in. Nice to see you.'

His mother appeared in the hallway as they entered, small and frail-looking in her thick fleshy tights and flowery housecoat. Her skin was pale and white and there were shadows around her rheumy eyes.

'Who is it, Martin?' she asked in a thin, whining voice,

her gaze sweeping nervously across the two of them. Martin, Colin thought. So that's his first name.

'It's just a couple of friends, mother,' Sefton explained tightly, ushering them into a front room.

'Oh,' she replied, as though he had said 'it's the milkman'. She was still wringing her hands uncertainly in the hallway when he closed the front room door on her.

'I'm glad to see you, Colin,' Sefton said seriously, gesturing at the settee and chairs. This was obviously the good room, clean and stale, with lace doillies over the backs of the furniture and little glass animals on the mantelpiece. 'I'm glad we haven't fallen out.' Colin shrugged.

'He was there when the shooting happened,' Hutchy announced, lowering himself into an armchair. He draped one leg carefully across an arm of the chair, as if to annoy Sefton. 'At the golf club.'

'Scum,' Sefton said softly, shaking his head as though baffled by the thing. 'It's hard to believe.' What are you baffled for, Colin thought, it's perfectly simple. You walk up to someone and you blow off half of their head. It's not complicated.

Sefton made coffee and brought in his guitar and Colin sat with it across his knees and picked out a few lilting blues riffs. The tone was good and it gave a form of life to the dead room. Sefton took his mug of coffee and stood at the window, staring out at the garden and the road. Hutchy fidgeted, bored.

'You get better at that every time I see you, Colin,' Sefton remarked.

'Practice, that's all. Lots of practice.'

'I hadn't though we'd see you back here again. I thought we might have fallen out.'

Colin played with the harmonics, letting the tiny notes ring in the air, saying nothing.

'You didn't seem to want to get involved.'

'I didn't want to get involved,' Colin said.

'So why are you back?'

'I've nothing better to do. I was hanging around with Hutchy and we took a dander up. I didn't know coming in through the door meant you'd joined up.'

'No, it doesn't.'

'Well, then.'

Sefton rubbed at his nose, unsure of what to say. 'You just seemed to have . . . what, moral objections to what we were doing?'

'Yeah. That's right.' He paused, glanced from one to the other. 'I phoned the confidential telephone, as a matter of fact.' Suddenly the silence became very loud between them. Hutchy was sitting very still in his chair, looking across in disbelief.

'You what?'

'I didn't say anything, I just put the phone down.'

'You're sure about that?' Sefton asked.

'Oh aye.'

Sefton came away from the window and set his mug down carefully on a side-table. All the colour seemed to have drained from his face. 'Why didn't you say any-thing?' he asked, trying to control the nerves in his voice.

'Ah, I don't know. Didn't want to get the big lad into trouble.' He smiled at Hutchy, who didn't smile back.

'This is serious, Colin,' Hutchy said, and there was a warning in his voice. 'I could go to jail.'

'You're all right, I didn't say anything.'

'That's not the point.'

'It's all right, Hutchy,' Sefton said quickly. He sat down on a straight-backed chair beside the window; the weak daylight fell on one side of his face and made his skin look cold, like wax. Colin began to strum a calypso on the guitar. He was happy at the reaction he had caused, frightening them like that. Make the pair of them sweat a bit, he thought, no bad thing. Sefton turned his head and stared out of the window into the scrubby front garden.

'We could still use you, Colin,' he said after a moment. 'There's still a place for you in the group. If ever you change your mind.'

'I've had enough of people being killed, thanks very much.'

'We're not planning to kill people.'

'What about the guns? What are they for, then? Gardening?'

'We're going to fight back. That doesn't necessarily mean killing people. It means fighting.'

'Where's the difference?'

Sefton shifted slightly, his expression unchanged. 'I think it's best if I explain exactly what we're about here, Colin,' he began slowly. 'Let me put it this way. If a man joins the army he becomes a soldier, right? And if he has to kill someone, in the course of his duty, that doesn't make him a murderer, does it?'

'So?'

'What I'm trying to say is that we have a purpose which I think you've missed. We're not just going out to murder people. We're fighting a war. There's a war out there, Colin; they're waging a war against us and the Government doesn't care. Do you think anyone is going to do anything out of the ordinary because Mullan has been killed? Of course not. They'll say how awful it is and they'll condemn his murder but they'll not do anything. They haven't got the will. So where does that leave us, Colin, mm? Where does that put the likes of you and me and Hutchy? We're targets, Colin, that's all. Targets. And those Fenian scum can drive across the border and wipe us out with impunity. They can do what they like because the Government doesn't care. Well, I care, Colin, I care, Hutchy cares. You'd be surprised how many people care enough to act.' He had clasped his hands together in his lap and now they were flexing and squirming in his excitement.

'We're taking the war back to them, Colin. If the authorities won't do it then we have to do it ourselves. We're going to fight them. And if we have to kill them, then we'll kill them, we'll send them to damnation for eternity. God knows we're entitled to defend ourselves. But they chose the game, Colin, never forget that; they chose the rules, so they can't crow if we kill a few in return. Their game. Mullan didn't choose the game. He wanted to be a policeman and they killed him for it. It wasn't his choice, it was theirs. Never forget that!'

He turned and looked out of the window again. A tiny bead of white spittle was hanging on his lower lip and Colin found himself staring at it as it bounced and bobbed.

'I'm a Christian, Colin,' he went on, staring out at the garden. 'You know how much I love the Lord. And the Lord knows I don't want to take up arms against his enemies, but I won't shirk that duty, Colin. I won't shirk it. Not me.'

He was silent for a long moment but still his hands rubbed and worked at each other. Colin glanced across at Hutchy who briefly rolled his eyes skyward, then began to strum out a slow, heavy twelve-bar blues on the bass strings. The thick, bouncing rhythm seemed to suit the grey afternoon, and again he wished he could sing the way those old Negroes could sing. Nobody sang the blues like them.

The golf club was closed until the funeral as a mark of respect so Colin had nowhere especially to be and he stayed in Sefton's house for an hour, playing the guitar and listening to what Sefton had to say. He tried to listen carefully but it all washed over him, like the surf over a black headland, leaving him surrounded and exposed. Later he walked with Hutchy to the Anchor Inn, just as darkness was beginning to settle around the town.

'You know who set Mullan up, don't you?' Hutchy asked him, as they walked side by side along the wide footpath.

'No. Who?'

'Your man the bar manager. Kelly.'

'Mr Kelly? Not a chance.'

'How do you know?'

'He liked Mullan. Mullan stood up for him at the club. They were mates. He wouldn't have set him up.'

'Well,' said Hutchy, his voice laden with certainty. 'That's who it was.'

They walked on in silence. The road led off before them, lined on both sides with a chain of yellow street-lights. The slight breeze was blowing the smoke down from the chimneys and Colin caught the sharp smell of coal.

'Who told you it was Kelly?' he asked after a while.

'Sefton has some friend in the cops. Apparently they've got all the evidence on him. Kelly set him up.'

'Nah,' Colin replied. 'No way. Not Kelly.'

But all the same the thought stayed in his mind and that night as he lay drunk in his bed with his head whirling around inside his skull and his stomach beginning to swoop and sway he considered it again. Kelly certainly knew that Mullan played golf every Saturday morning, he would have been ideally placed to pass on information. You never know, he thought slowly, beginning to drift into sleep; you never bloody well know.

Stevie had been awake in the darkened bedroom when the two boys arrived outside the house, singing 'The Sash My Father Wore' tunelessly at the top of their voices. He smiled to himself as he recognised his son's voice raised in the chorus. That'll give the neighbours something to complain about, he thought warmly. They were chanting the words rather than singing them, a harsh, aggressive and frightening sound, and just for a second he recalled the thrill of a flute band on the Twelfth of July, with the flutes blowing and the snare-drums rattling and the swagger of thirty men all in step with something righteous to fight about. It was good music, fighting music, music to make the blood boil. By Christ, he thought, we had some good times in those days. Singing around the bonfires on the eleventh night. Belonging.

The two lads shouted their goodbyes in the street and he heard Colin fumbling and scraping at the lock, trying to get the key in. Hutchy wandered off up the street, still singing. A right big lad, that Hutchy, Stevie thought; he'd known a lot like him. Strong and steady and a wee bit thick, but with his heart in the right place. Not like that fellow Sefton. I've known a lot like him, as well, Stevie reminded himself. They were the graspers, the fiddlers, the men who filled the young lads' heads full of rubbish then sent them out to murder, and they were more guilty than anyone. He hadn't worried that much when Mullan was around, because Mullan would have controlled it; he would have watched and waited and, just before things went too far, he would have stepped in and fixed it. He was a good man, Mullan. Stevie wondered briefly where he had gone to, where his spirit was. That was a terrible way to die, too, though, shot down like a dog. Then again, he thought, is there a nice way to die?

He listened as Colin rattled about in the kitchen, then followed the thudding footsteps as he slouched up the stairs to his bedroom. Beside him Angie stirred and mumbled in her sleep.

This was a bad time for the boy because of the shooting. Seeing that sort of thing for the first time unbalanced you, it knocked you off-centre until you managed to get your feet square on the ground again. This was the time Sefton would be trying to get his claws into the boy, luring him in. It was a dangerous time. But there was no point talking to him, because anything you said could send him the wrong way. You just had to be there for him and hope he made the right choice.

Stevie had often wondered what he would do if Colin turned out bad. Many times in the past he had beaten the boy harder and longer than he deserved, trying to instil some sort of fearful goodness into him, or perhaps beat the evil out of him. He was afraid that badness ran in the blood, that it was a disease carried from father to son, generation to generation. If that was true then there was no way out and the boy would follow his father's path into crime. More than anything in his life Stevie did not want that to happen. He thought there must be something to say or do but he couldn't imagine what; every time he went to speak to the boy his mouth clammed up and his brain seized and the worry came over him again, washing everything else away.

Colin was humming to himself in the other room as he got undressed for bed. At least he'll sleep tonight, Stevie thought. He sounds drunk enough for ten men. And Angie will scold him in the morning and he'll have a hangover and he'll feel just like a real man, and it'll probably do him good. The boy needed sleep. Stevie knew just how hard it was to sleep after seeing something like that. Unbidden, his mind flew back to a crowded, smokey club in a street off the Shankill and a spray of blood spattering on the cheap flock wallpaper, and he found himself shuddering. Next door the springs creaked in Colin's bed as the boy landed under the duvet. Sleep well, Stevie thought. Sleep well and pleasant dreams.

Mullan was originally from some small town in the country and they held the funeral there, in a neat grey stone church set back among trees. It was too far for Colin to travel so he watched it on the television in Hutchy's house. There was some scandal about a politician so it didn't make the national news but they caught it on the local bulletin; they showed the cards arriving at the church gates and a black-gloved policeman snapping his hand to salute and the family holding on to each other as they stepped into the church. Mullan's wife looked much thinner on the TV. She was weeping into a small lace hanky with a black border around it. Colin wondered briefly did all such families keep black bordered hankies in the bottom of their drawers, just in case?

'Is that his daughter?' Hutchy, asked, pointing at a pale girl in a dark grey suit.

'Don't know, Hutch.'

157

'Nice bit of stuff,' Hutchy said, wiggling his toes in his socks.

'That's his wife,' Colin remarked, pointing her out.

'Nah, I wouldn't be interested in her. Too old.'

From the kitchen came the whoosh of chips dropping into hot oil as Mrs Hutchinson made the tea. On the news the minister was speaking about the murder. '. . . absolutely heinous crime. One fails to comprehend what new depths of depravity these men can stoop to . . .'

The Minister of State for Security came on, looking tired and sorrowful. '. . . I can promise you here and now that the men of violence will not win . . .'

'They are winning, you stupid bastard,' Hutchy snapped.

The anger began as the shock subsided, Colin had decided. Immediately afterwards there had been no room for anything but the shock; a nightmare had slipped into his reality, and the mind needed time to deal with that. But the shock gradually settled, like disturbed sand in a puddle of sea-water, drifting on to the bottom and leaving the water clear, and as the mind cleared the anger settled in. More and more Colin found himself thinking about the man who had pulled the trigger, about all the tiny details which were starting to come flooding back; the way he walked, the way he dressed, the number of pockets on his jacket. He had seen the same jacket for sale in a shop in Coleraine. The way the gun had jerked upwards each time he fired. The more he considered it the more angry he became, because the killer had no justice; he was just a man, same as any other, he bought his jackets in a cheap clothes shop, he wore polished DM boots, his jeans were turned up at the bottom. He had no more right to decide who should live and who should die than Colin had. He was just another man and he had killed a friend and the anger was beginning.

There was another funeral taking place, in Keady of a UDR man who had been killed in a boobytrap bomb. Hutchy leaned forward and stabbed at the remote control.

'We might get it on the ITV news,' he said. The other channel covered it from a different angle but with most of the same shots. Mullan's daughter was tasty, Colin had to admit.

'There's Piper!' Hutchy sputtered suddenly. 'Look, there he is!'

'Where?'

'Ah, he's away now, you've missed him. Old Piper. He wasn't in uniform or anything. Must have just been going to the funeral.'

'He might have offered us a lift,' Colin said sourly.

'Ay,' Hutchy said. 'Right enough.' He heaved himself off the floor and on to the settee, scratching his finger around inside his nostril. 'Bastards,' he said shortly.

'Who?'

'Politicians. They don't give a shit about us. They've got their jobs. If there was peace tomorrow they'd all lose their jobs.'

The smell of sausages and chips and hot oil was drifting through from the kitchen, and Colin felt his stomach gurgling from hunger. 'I'd better go,' he said, standing up. 'You'll be getting your dinner soon.'

'You can get some if you want. The old dear'll put some more chips on.'

'Nah. I promised Stevie I'd be home.'

Hutchy shrugged. 'All right,' he said. 'By the way, Sefton asked me to tell you. He's having a prayer meeting at his house tomorrow night. Said you could come if you want.'

'Jesus Christ, Hutchy, what would I do at a prayer meeting?'

'It's not a real prayer meeting,' Hutchy said softly, glancing around the living room. 'That's just what he calls it. It's a training session.' He looked archly at Colin.

'Oh,' Colin said. 'Stupid name for it.'

'Code. Security, very important.' Hutchy tapped his finger importantly along the side of nose. 'Tomorrow night, seven o'clock. Be there or be square.'

There was a fellow called Brian who was to do the instructing and he was short and heavy with a pale blue polo shirt pulled taut by his gut. He seemed short of breath, and after he spoke he flicked his tongue around his lips to moisten them. Colin was reminded of lizards in wildlife programmes.

'This here is the, ah . . .' The tongue flicked out round the mouth. 'The bolt. There's your firing pin.' He poked a squat finger at one end of the bolt. 'That's the bit that hits the cartridge.'

Sefton had pulled the kitchen table into the middle of the floor and had laid a pale cream blanket over the top of it; the machine-gun was now lying in pieces on the blanket. Brian stood behind the table and the three of them, Colin, Sefton and Hutchy, sat around on hard-backed chairs, watching. The yellow light from the ceiling lamp cast dull shadows in the corners. It *was* a bit like a prayer meeting, Colin reflected. Brian had a thick moustache which hung untidily over his mouth and caught small beads of spit.

'It goes in like this – ' he held the tip of his tongue between his teeth while fitting the bolt inside the body of the gun and letting it drop home ' – and you let it slide down in there. Like that.'

There were two of the machine-guns and two of the pistols. The machine-guns were Swedish, according to Brian; they had folding stocks and magazines which fitted into the bottom of the body. They were dark grey-black in colour, heavy-looking and oily inside, and where the metal had been rubbed and worn the steel glinted cleanly.

'There's two of these magazines with each gun,' Brian was saying, holding up one of the magazines. 'You can get thirty rounds in each one but you shouldn't use more than about twenty-five. If you put in too many you'll get jams.' Tongue around the mouth again. His hair was gingery blond in colour, and the thin matting on his freckled forearms looked repulsive. Colin was waiting to get his hands on the guns themselves. He had never held a machine-gun before.

Brian was having trouble getting the cocking handle back into the hole in the bolt; he was pushing and shoving at it, his face reddening with the exertion and the embarrassment. I suppose he likes to be the expert, Colin thought. He wondered idly what Sefton had done with his mother for the evening, and for a moment he entertained an amusing image of the old girl tied up and gagged on one of the beds.

'How far away can you be when you shoot the thing?'

Hutchy asked. He was leaning forward intently, watching everything, taking it all in.

'You need to get up to about ten or twelve feet. If you're any further away you'll hit nothing – ' the cocking handle suddenly slid home. 'There. That's that. No, about twelve feet. You don't want to waste ammo.'

'That's a bit close, isn't it?'

'That's where you've got to be. Otherwise you'll miss.'

The man who killed Mullan had been within arm's length of his victim. Colin saw again the blood spattering on the inside of the rear window and the upturned cloth cap filling with blood. He had fantasised about finding the fellow who did it; he spent long minutes contriving impossible tortures and means of execution. There would be no qualms at all about killing him, none whatsoever. If they wheeled him into this kitchen, now, he would put a gun to his head and pull the trigger and it wouldn't worry him a bit. Like Sefton said, they picked the game, and they can't complain if we start to play by their rules. It was all very logical and proper.

'And make sure you load the bullets in the right way round,' Brian said. 'There was a fellow in Magherafelt had a whole magazine loaded with the rounds back-to-front.'

'What happened?' Sefton asked.

'Click. Nothing happened. The peelers lifted him. Silly bastard.' Brian chuckled coarsely and Sefton winced slightly at the crudeness. He was sitting very properly in the centre with his legs crossed neatly and his arms folded, watching with the sort of detached interest that made you think he would never actually handle the guns. He wasn't the type for it, anyway, Colin thought.

Too prim and tidy, too clean. A good planner, though. That was his niche; planning.

Brian handed them the two machine-guns and Colin and Hutchy tried to take them apart and put them together again. Hutchy didn't hold on to the end-cap properly and the mainspring forced it off, sending parts shooting into the air and they called a brief halt to the lesson while the floor of the kitchen was searched for the firing pin. Colin got the hang of it in no time at all, slapping the cocking handle back like a professional. It felt really good to be armed, to have a real weapon tucked into your shoulder. To squint through real sights. It made you feel powerful. He imagined Mullan's killer standing in front of him and he lined up with the head and pulled the trigger. The heavy bolt crashed home with a satisfying clunk.

Sefton played half-heartedly with the two machine-guns and then they went on to the pistols. These were much more attractive than the bigger weapons; they seemed to have a tightness about them as they lay on the table, like a watch-spring coiled up small. They were smooth and cold and heavy, shining under the bare yellow light. One was a Browning Hi-Power and the other was a squat-looking revolver with a short barrel and rounded wooden grips.

'This is a Taurus .38,' Brian announced, opening the cylinder and spinning it. 'Takes six rounds. They're not the same as for the other guns, so don't get them mixed up. And you've only got twenty rounds for it, so don't waste them.'

The pistols were great. Colin waved the Hi-Power around the room, watching over the sights. The butt was thick and solid in his grip. After a while Brian seemed to get bored and Sefton decided to make a pot of tea. They drank the tea in the kitchen with the weapons lying on the table between them.

'They're not as complicated as they look,' Brian was saying dully, peering down into his teacup. Colin reckoned he'd have rather had a beer. 'You'll pick it up in no time.'

'What about rifles?' Hutchy asked.

'Let's see how you get on with these first. Then we can talk about rifles.'

Sefton never talked about the 'organisation' except to stress how secure it was or how far-reaching it was. As far as Colin understood, the three of them constituted a cell. Sefton was the cell leader. Brian was the next man up the line after Sefton, and he was in charge of three or four or five cells. But none of them knew about any of the others. Sefton claimed the system had the true simplicity of all great ideas, but Colin reckoned the vagueness surrounding it all was intended to mask the massive gaps. He didn't really believe there were five or six other cells. One maybe, or two. No more than that. And all right, so they had produced guns, well, big deal. There must be thousands of illegal guns in Northern Ireland. Probably the best-armed community in the world. There seemed to be a lot of wishful thinking going on. Then again, what did it matter, as long as they had the guns and could strike back. You had to start somewhere, after all.

They worked on for another hour and eventually Brian lost interest and he and Sefton went over by the sink and spoke together in quiet tones, leaving Colin and Hutchy to play with the weapons. Colin took the Browning apart and reassembled it slowly, running his hands over the smooth steel, enjoying the coldness of the machined barrel, the neat click and clatter as the parts fitted together. There was a purpose in a gun which ran all the way though it, from the chequered plastic grips to the neat serrations on the trigger to the shining steel of the barrel, a completeness, as if all the component parts were a perfect team working to a perfect goal. He pulled back the slide and let it go, leaving the hammer cocked. He wished he could fire it once or twice before they actually used the gun; just one or two rounds, to get the feel of it. With the hammer cocked and the springs compressed inside the weapon felt taut and dangerous, and with a sudden flight of wildness Colin swung round in the chair and, holding the gun out at arm's length, pointed it at Brian's forehead. Sefton had been talking and he stopped immediately, starting up slightly. Brian's face drained of colour and just for a second his eyes closed, as if in some brief and final prayer, then he remembered that there were no bullets in the pistol and his face flushed.

'Bang!' said Colin.

'Don't you ever do that again, you wee cunt!' Brian's face was bright red, a mixture of embarrassment and rage.

'Aw, lighten up, would you,' Colin said, turning away. He was about to set the pistol back on to the table when Brian's hand shot out and slapped him hard across the cheek, jerking his head sideways.

'Don't you fucking mess about with me!' he snapped, his voice hoarse and cracking. Colin was still for a second and the child in him flashed across his mind and disappeared, then he swept up the pistol again and swung it round hard, rising from the chair at the same time. Brian was settling back to lean against the sink again, satisfied that he had preserved his honour when the butt of the heavy pistol slammed into his forehead. His eyes opened wide with the shock of it but his body was too slow to react and Colin brought his knee up hard, not aiming but hoping and pleased when it sank into something soft and fat. Sefton had jumped to one side, squealing at Hutchy to do something. Colin heard Hutchy laughing, and he swung the pistol across the fat man's face once again and then stepped back to the far side of the room.

Brian was crouched over with one hand at his face and the other clutching at his injured genitals. He was hissing with anger, not looking towards Colin. Hutchy was leaning back in his chair, sniggering happily. Sefton was pale and affronted.

'Don't you ever slap me again,' Colin said, panting from the adrenalin surge. 'Or I'll come after you.'

Brain looked up at Sefton. 'He's fucking mad, that one! He's a fucking nut case!'

Sefton's mouth opened once or twice but nothing came out. It seemed to Colin that the whole atmosphere of the room had changed, now they were all at different corners and waiting for the next move. He tossed the pistol on to the blanketed table.

'Fuck it. I'm away. I'll see you tomorrow, Hutchy.'

'Aye. Cheerio, Colin.'

As he walked out into the cold night air he felt strangely happy, still high from the pumping thrill of sudden violence. They were a bunch of old women, he reckoned. The man Brian had thought he was a big fellow, well he wasn't so bloody big now. It had felt supremely good to bring him down a peg or two. He wouldn't be so quick to slap people round the head now.

He walked down on to the shadows of Pottinger's Alley, which led along behind the buildings on the seafront, then cut through on to the promenade and along the front of the shops. There were only two or three kids sitting in cars along the front, and as he walked past them Colin felt himself almost growing and swelling and gaining in power, until he could contain it no longer and gave a mighty, roaring yell into the night air. 'Yeeee-hawwww!' he shouted, letting it split the night. Across the road an old woman jerked her head around and looked at him for a short while, then shook her head sadly and lumbered on back to her home.

The golf club opened again the day after the funeral but hardly anyone came in, perhaps all afraid of the too-recent ghost who might be lurking in the car-park. Those who did play a few holes were sombre and reserved, and played their game as a form of respect for their departed colleague. No one came into the bar, and no one booked a table in the restaurant.

Barry spent the day wandering around the deserted building, from his office to the bar, then to the kitchen, then back to the office again. He went once to the professional's shop but the three men there, who had been talking in low tones, stopped talking completely when he came in and stood looking significantly at each other until he left again. He knew two of them well enough to greet, but they made no sign of it. They think I did it, he realised.

It was understandable in a way but that didn't make it right, and the injustice of it hurt him. He had done nothing wrong, and he was being punished. Probably in a month or two it would be forgotten and things would be back to normal again, but a month was a long time and if someone took his case back to the Committee the decision might not go his way a second time. Now they assumed he was the enemy. There were several members who were in the police or UDR, and probably more whom he didn't know, and they would certainly keep away from him. For them the club would have become a place of risk, a dangerous place. In a month they might forget, but in a month they might be asking for his removal. And the awful thing was that he couldn't blame them.

Ernie James and Colin Rea were on the early shift, and they were both in strange form. Ernie was sitting on a crate behind the bar staring into space, while the boy Colin was polishing glasses and stacking bottles and doing everything and anything he could find to do. Barry had worried about the effect the killing would have on the boy. He had known a young fellow in the Bogside who had seen his uncle shot dead in his living room; he had been one of those sensitive, artistic types, but the murder had thrown him totally off-centre and he had shuffled about for a year before throwing himself off the bridge into the Foyle. A murder was like a stone thrown into a quiet lake; it wasn't just the plunk as the stone sank into the water, it was the ripples which slid quietly out in running circles, upsetting the flotsam around the lake edge and rebounding to cross themselves in intricate patterns.

After lunch a delivery of beer arrived and the two barmen helped to roll and carry the steel kegs down into the cellar. Barry stood by and watched. Normally he would have joined in and lent a hand, but there was something in the quiet way the two men went about it which told him he was not welcome. He stood for a while, watching, listening to the clang and scrape of the kegs on the cobbles and the panting of the barmen as they hauled them down the cellar steps.

'Y'is are all very quiet today,' the driver remarked, standing up on the flat bed of the truck with his thick-gloved hands swinging by his side. Maybe he didn't hear about it, Barry thought.

'Just one of those days,' he replied.

The police arrived in the afternoon, two detectives in heavy overcoats and brightly polished shoes. They took Barry into his office.

'When was the last time you saw Dermot Lavin?' the tall one asked without preamble. They were standing by the door, their coats still on, their attitude hostile.

'I told you all this already.'

'Just answer the question.'

'At a party, last week. My brother's house.'

'Have you seen him since?'

'No.'

'Was there anyone with him?'

'No. I don't think so. I didn't notice.'

The tall policeman sat down in the armchair beside the desk, hoisting up his trousers and crossing his legs carefully.

'I have to tell you, Mr Kelly, that we have evidence which points to Lavin being centrally involved in Mullan's killing. Now, you've already admitted you know him. More than that, you saw him a matter of days before the murder was carried out. That connects you to him. I reckon we could probably hang a charge on that, if we had to. We might not get a conviction, but it would definitely go as far as court.'

If he was involved in a murder case as a suspect then he could kiss his career goodbye, unless he wanted to spend the rest of his days serving stolen beer in Republican shebeens. Barry felt his palms dampening.

'Think about that for a moment, Mr Kelly,' the other one said. 'Think about how that would affect your career.'

'The thing is, we don't know where Lavin is at the minute. He's on the run. He's in Derry somewhere, we know that, and we're taking a quiet look at a few houses just to see who pops up, but it would save us a lot of time and trouble if we could go straight to him and pick him up.'

'I don't know where he is.'

'Think about it, Mr – '

'Honestly, I don't. I've only seen him once in five years, and I was half-drunk at the time. I don't know where he is.'

'We're talking about a murderer here, Mr Kelly. A killer. And he isn't going to stop at one. He's going to kill more people. Innocent people. There's someone out there now, walking around, living their life, kissing their kids good-night. Looking forward to Christmas. Someone who Lavin is going to kill next. Do you want that to happen? Do you want innocent blood on your hands? I wouldn't want that, Mr Kelly, I wouldn't want to have to live with that thought for the rest of my life. To think that a man died because I wouldn't tell the truth.'

'I am telling the truth,' he whimpered. He jammed his elbows on to the desk and rested his face in his palms. He didn't want the policemen to see him cry. It's not fair, he thought, it just isn't fair, I didn't ask for this. 'I don't know anything. Honestly.' He gulped air in, tried to keep his chest from heaving. The two detectives watched without emotion. This is what they want, Barry thought, they want me to break down, they want me to blub out everything I know.

'Are you looking forward to Christmas, Mr Kelly?' the tall one asked after a while. Barry nodded dumbly, keeping his face in his hands.

'So was Julie Mullan. She'd already got her father his Christmas present, you know. She knit him an Aran pullover. She was crying the other night because he's never going to see it. Ever.'

'Where is Lavin, Mr Kelly?'

'I don't know where he is. If I knew I would tell you.'

'You could find out though, couldn't you?'

'If he's hiding somewhere, he's hardly likely to tell everyone, is he?'

'Oh, just a word here and there. You'd be surprised how hard it is to keep a secret these days. You could make a few enquiries for us.'

'They'd kill me.'

'No.'

'Yes they would. You bloody well know they would.'

The tall one shifted in his seat. He pushed his fingertips together to make a cage and peered into it. 'Look, we don't want to charge you. You're small fry. We're after Lavin. But I'll tell you this, Kelly, for nothing; somebody is going down for Mullan's murder. We're going to make damn sure of that. Now, if we get Lavin, then he'll be the one, and we'll not be interested in you. But if we don't get him, I'm sorry to say that you're the next on the list. And we'll work and work until we have enough to hang you with, I can promise you that. So my advice is this; find out where Lavin is, and let us know. That's the only sensible thing to do.'

It was all too much and he couldn't hold the pain anymore and he let himself go, his frame jerking and shaking with the massive sobs, the tears trickling through his fingers and dripping on to the green blotter.

'I don't know anything,' he sobbed. 'Honest to God I don't.'

'Well, you'd better find something out quick, then, hadn't you?' the tall one said. They both went out and left him alone in the room, weeping and crying like a beaten child.

When he wasn't working in the golf club Colin spent his time at Sefton's house, or hiding up in his bedroom playing with the guitar. He spent a long time trying to get a particular riff from a Guns and Roses album, but there was a run in it he couldn't work out and in the end he gave up. He ate his meals in silence and his mother worried about him. Sometimes he would hear her arguing with Stevie down in the living room, and he knew they were arguing about him. He didn't like to hurt them, but there just didn't seem to be anything to say. He was moving in a different world now. He had seen death and he was learning how to fight and the old family tensions were no longer of importance to him. He was a giant, strolling through weeds.

He didn't tell them that he went to Sefton's house; he always said he was going over to Hutchy's, or down to the arcade, or sometimes just out for a walk. It became almost a game, thinking of excuses and trying to remember them, always having to fit the stories together. There were occasional slips but no one had seemed to notice. He didn't like lying to his mother, though: he didn't care about Stevie because Stevie would kill him if he discovered the truth and it was just self-preservation, but he thought his mother deserved better and he didn't like it.

On the second Tuesday after Mullan's murder his mother made roast beef and cabbage and boiled potatoes and the three of them ate in silence, listening only to the tiny clinking of the cutlery on the plates and the background whirr of the refrigerator. Even the television in the living room was switched off. Now and again Stevie snuffled or coughed. When Angie finished the meal she placed her knife and fork down on her empty plate, very gently, and clasped her hands under her chin. Colin knew this as a sign of concern.

'Are you all right, Colin?' she asked quietly. He looked up briefly from his plate.

'Yeah, I'm fine.'

'You've been very quiet lately.'

'Ah. Just having one of those weeks, you know.'

'Your father and I were a wee bit worried about you.'

'Well, there's nothing to worry about.'

He felt like a dog growling over his food. Stevie was watching him carefully, with that old argumentative look in his eye. Don't start now, for God's sake, Colin thought.

'Where are you going tonight?' he asked gruffly.

'Just round to Hutchy's house.'

'But you were round at Hutchy's last night.'

176

'I only get two nights off in a week; tomorrow I'm back at work. All right?'

Angie was watching him too and she looked tense and worried and Colin began to think that there was maybe something behind all the concern. He looked back at the old man's face and caught the hardness there and was suddenly frightened.

'Look, what is this?' he asked.

'You weren't at Hutchy's last night,' Stevie said evenly. 'You never went there at all.'

'I did.'

'Don't make this worse by lying to me, son.'

He looked at his mother again and she wouldn't meet his eyes and the atmosphere was cooling by the second. Colin felt the anger coming back again.

'It's nothing to you where I went, anyhow,' he said.

'I'm your father.'

'You're a stupid old git.'

He had said it before he realised. Stevie rose quickly and smoothly, hitting his thighs against the table and knocking over the bottle of HP sauce. He stood upright, his arms bent slightly, his eyes glaring. Colin jerked nervously backwards in his chair, waiting for the punch.

'Sit down, Stevie, please,' Angie whispered.

'You were at Sefton's house, weren't you?' Stevie demanded.

'I was at Hutchy's.'

'You were fucking not!' Stevie roared, suddenly reaching out and sweeping Colin's plate on to the floor. Colin leapt out of his seat, knocking over the chair, jumping slightly to avoid it. He swallowed heavily.

'Stephen!' Angie cried uselessly, holding her hands to

her face and backing off towards the door. She could feel the anger in the air. Colin glanced towards her and saw the fear in her eyes and it fuelled his rage; that old bastard had no right to frighten her like that. No right at all.

'Didn't I warn you not to go near him?' Stevie hissed.

'It's got nothing to do with you where I go or who I see.'

'Is that right?'

Even with his bad leg Stevie was fast and the right arm flashed out and caught Colin squarely on the cheekbone. It was like being hit by a block of wood. His head snapped to the side and he fell back against the kitchen units. He heard Angie scream. He was surprised to see tiny lights dancing behind his eyelids. So this is seeing stars, he thought, opening his eyes in time to see the next blow coming, this time an open-handed slap across the face which cracked like a rifle shot. His cheek stung wildly and he was knocked down on to the lino, banging his head hard on the front of the cooker. Stevie was on him again, grabbing at the front of his T-shirt and pulling him upwards, wincing at the pain in his bad leg. His eyes were cold and frightening, pale, with no warmth at all.

'You did it!' Colin grabbed. 'You did it, just the same as me! I'm only doing what you did!'

'Aye, I did it, all right. God help me. I did it.' Another swinging slap and Colin felt his teeth cutting into the flesh of his mouth and the warm salty taste of blood.

'Leave me alone!' he shouted.

'You're a stupid wee bastard!'

'Leave me alone, fuck you!'

The next blow was coming straight for his nose and he dodged to one side and let it past, slipping round to unbalance his father, pulling him on to his weak leg. Stevie yelled with pain and fell against the cupboards, and Colin shook himself free and hooked his foot behind the one good leg. Stevie twisted out of it in time and dragged himself upright and was drawing back to swing again when Colin hit him with all the strength he had, grunting with the effort, pushing his fist into his father's face. He felt bone under skin. Blood spurted from the old man's nose, and he fell backwards and on to the floor, grabbing at the bad leg as it twisted beneath him.

Colin stood with his fists bunched ready for more, panting for breath, his heart hammering, terrified. The old man rolled over on to his side, his face contorted with pain, blood streaming down his upper lip. A few drops of blood fell on to the lino, landing in big red inky spots. He had never seen his father in so much pain before. He was an old man. This was his blood. Something like this could kill him.

Angie ran across and went down to help him, weeping and sobbing, her hair across her face and strands of it dampened by the tears. Stevie was clutching at his bad knee, his eyes still closed, his face tightened and wrinkled and white, terribly, dreadfully white. He was a vicious old bastard but he was still Colin's father and after all you only got the one.

'Is he all right?'

'I don't know,' Angie sobbed.

Then, as if his mouth had suddenly been freed, Stevie yelled with the pain and it was a terrible, frightening scream of pain. He's dying, Colin thought. He's an old man and I've just beaten him up and he's dying now. Maybe I've broken his leg again, or something. Angie was trying to get him into a sitting position, pulling at his shirt, hoisting him upwards like a sack of cement and all the time weeping and sobbing. Colin felt suddenly that he had no place there, that this was no longer his home, that these two injured people would be better off without him. He gulped down a few breaths then turned and, snatching up his jacket, sprinted out of the back door and ran on into the night.

He ran for the first mile and then began to walk, following the long, sloping winding road down to the beach, with the wind rustling the dry grasses on the banks of each side. There were no cars on the beach and once he got on to the long flat expanse of sand he began to jog along, letting the tears run down his face and cool his cheeks in the night breeze. The old man had no right to act like that. There was nothing Colin was doing that Stevie hadn't done twice as much of when they lived in Belfast. Colin remembered men coming furtively to the house with heavy, clanking sports-bags, the nights when he and his mother were sent over to his aunt's house because the men wanted some secrecy. The big polythene bag full of dull brass rifle bullets hidden below the stairs. Stevie had been a leader then, an organiser. How could he turn round now and say it was wrong?

The old man had screamed, though. Colin had never heard a scream like that before, and especially not from Stevie. You never expected your father to scream. Christ, it must have hurt him. And what if it was broken again?

They had all lived with the bad leg for ten years and although they had bickered and cursed about it, there had still been much pain for the old man. It was awful to think that he might have to go through all that again, just because Colin lost his temper. He wished he had never heard of Sefton, or Mullan for that matter, he wished he had never been angry. It would have been easier to keep quiet and take the blows.

He turned off the beach and into the dunes, slipping and falling on the soft sand. There was a dune which rose to a sudden ridge before falling sixty feet into a sandy valley. You could hide in the grass on top and see the length of the beach, from the rocks near the town to the distant estuary of the Bann and further, to the smooth greed hills of Donegal. Colin headed towards it, jogging easily along the paths of his childhood and scrabbling up the steep path to the top. He had often come here with Hutchy and they had thrown themselves down the steep sandy cliff, tumbling over and over in a cloud of dry sand until finally bouncing against each other in the centre of the valley, laughing and shouting at the wildness of their descent. It was all a long time ago, he thought, dropping heavily into the beach grass at the top of the ridge.

The beach was quiet; he could hear only his breathing and the gentle whoosh of the sea. The wind carried occasional snatches of traffic noise from the town, and when he shifted his position he heard his clothes rustle. He lay on his stomach and gazed out across the pale surf at the blackness of the sea, letting the chill of the sand seep into his stomach and chest, feeling the reality of it. Nothing had seemed real over the past few weeks.

181

Mullan being killed, Sefton and his guns. Stevie lying in agony in the kitchen. It seemed that the world had gone mad on him. At least the sea never changed. It was always there, every morning and every night, coming in and going out, reliable. No matter what anyone did, nothing would stop that.

He looked out at the sea and the paler black of the sky above it and listened to the wind in the dry spiky grass and felt the cold of the sand through his shirt, and for a short while he felt that he was clean again.

He stayed on the beach all night, curled up in a sandy hollow with his head resting on his forearm and he slept a deep and dreamless sleep. He woke as the first glimmers of daylight were paling the eastern sky, shivering, his neck sore and aching from the way he had been lying, but he felt more refreshed than he had done for the past two weeks. He peered over the edge of the hollow and the sea was grey and the sand was pale fawn and the tide was in, breaking on the beach in waves of the cleanest, purest, freshest foam he had ever seen.

He sat for a while in the shelter of the hollow, rubbing at his eyes. There was sand in his hair and all up one side of his clothes, and the damp had soaked his jacket and trousers. You asshole, he thought, staying out here all night like a tramp. And yet he felt easier now than he had for a long time. So this is how tramps feel, he reflected. Not too bad, really, apart from the cold.

He had to make a decision and there were two choices: he could go back home and see if Stevie was all right and face the music for staying out all night, or he could go to Sefton's house and hide for a while. If he went to Hutchy's place they would phone his parents and tell them where he was, and it was somehow important that they didn't know that until he was ready to tell them.

It was a difficult decision because so much seemed to rest on it; he had an odd feeling of being at a crossroads and examining the signs, knowing that whatever road he chose he would have to follow to the end. He had not yet gone so far that he couldn't go back, but that point was not much further up ahead and he had to consider it now. There was no reason to feel that way, other than a nagging instinct that this day would somehow be important to him, but he felt inclined to trust his instinct. He sat for a long while in the hollow and then, undecided, he stood up and walked back up to the top of the high dune and stood for a moment, smelling the sea air and gazing up and down the pale length of the strand. In the distance he could hear the sound of early morning traffic coming from the direction of the town. I'm a king, he thought. A king and a fool. Six in the morning and I'm standing on the top of a sand-dune and the world is still grinding on.

He brushed off as much sand as he could and ran his fingers through his hair and adjusted the hang of his jacket. The steep, sloping sand-dune stretched downwards before him, clean and undisturbed, almost painfully smooth. Probably no one's been here since the summer, Colin thought. He remembered the games he and Hutchy had played years before. The clean sand beckoned. Oh, to hell with it, he thought, one last time. He lay down on the top and held his arms tight across his chest and pushed himself off, tumbling on to the sand with a jolt and rolling, gaining speed, gasping at the cold hardness of the sand as he bounced, rolling and rolling until he was going too fast to stop, out of control, sand flying into his face and hair, eyes tight shut and shouting, yelling wordlessly at the top of his voice at the wild, bouncing freedom of his ride.

Sefton had just got out of bed by the looks of him, but he brought Colin in and sat him in the kitchen and made him coffee and toast.

'What are you doing here at this hour of the morning?' he asked.

'I stayed out all night,' Colin replied. 'I slept on the beach.'

'Good Lord.'

'I had a fight with Stevie last night.'

'What about?'

'You, basically.'

'Oh, I see.'

Sefton was wearing thick striped pyjamas with a dark red dressing-gown which looked to be just a size too small. His feet were thrust into old mock-leather carpet slippers, and the skin of his heels was white and pale and sickly, mapped with pale blue veins.

'Well,' he said, sitting down at the table. 'You're always welcome here. You know that.'

'Yeah. Thanks.'

'I was worried about you, you know. I wasn't sure if you were totally committed. We need commitment, you see, Colin, we need dedication. What we're going to do won't be easy and you can't just back out of it when it gets tough.'

'You don't need to worry about that.'

'I just never heard you actually declare it, that's all.'

'Declare it?'

'Say that you're with us.'

Colin shrugged. Do I want to be a terrorist, he wondered? Sefton certainly had the answers. And at least Sefton wasn't beating him up every two days. 'I'm with you,' he said evenly.

Sefton smiled at him. 'Good,' he said casually, sipping at his own coffee. 'I'm glad we've got that settled. Now we can talk business. We've been authorised to carry out our first operation.'

Colin felt a thrill of excitement shiver through his body. 'When?' he asked.

'Soon as we can. They've given me some photographs of Republicans in the area. We'll pick one. Watch him. Decide on a plan, then carry out the operation.'

'Who's going to do it?'

'I haven't decided that yet.'

Sefton sent Colin down to the town to fetch milk and bread and to keep him out of the way while his mother had breakfast. Colin went into the coffee shop on the promenade and ordered a tea. He was their first customer of the morning and he had to wait while they

186

opened up the till. By the time he returned to Sefton's house his mother had dressed and gone off somewhere.

'Here are the photographs,' Sefton said, tossing a large brown envelope on to the table-top. He seemed more relaxed and confident with his mother out of the house. 'Have a look.'

They were mugshots, full face, each with the name and address typewritten below, arranged in three lines on a sheet of paper which had been photocopied. The faces weren't too clear but the addresses were legible. There were marks at the top and bottom where someone had obliterated some text.

'Where did these come from?'

'Never you mind. They're all known terrorists, though.'

'Oh. Which one do we hit first?

'I haven't decided yet.'

Stevie dressed himself carefully, trying not to move the bad leg as he pulled on his trousers. He had not had pain like that for a long while, since the hospital. Christ, but it had hurt. He was afraid that the fall might have broken some of the metal pins the surgeons had used to hold the bones together, but after groping tenderly at the whole length of it he had found no sign of any looseness beneath the skin. But still it had hurt. The way it had hurt when he came round in the hospital, just after the bomb, with tubes and tapes and white-coats all round the bed fussing at him and the maddening, white-hot pain stabbing suddenly at his legs.

He wasn't mad at the boy. He would have done the same in Colin's place and that was the terrible thing about it. In fact, he wouldn't have suffered it for so long, if the truth were to be told. If his father had treated him the way he treated Colin, he would have cracked him one long before this. The lad was just following his instincts.

Angie came in to the bedroom as he was buttoning up his shirt. 'Colin's bed hasn't been slept in,' she announced.

'So?'

'So where is he?'

'He'll be in someone's house. Don't worry about him.'

'What do you mean, don't worry about him? God knows where he is! Anything could have happened to him!'

'He's not stupid. He's just cooling off.'

She sat on the bed beside him, gnawing at her lower lip. She thought Colin was still a baby, that was her trouble. She thought he was still fourteen. 'If you hadn't started all that business about this Sefton character,' she began after a moment.

'Wait a minute,' Stevie retorted. 'I thought we'd agreed about that.'

'I didn't think you were going to beat him up!'

'I didn't beat him up!'

'You were going to!'

Stevie hobbled to the chest of drawers and snatched out the first pullover that came to hand, leaning against the cabinet to pull it on. 'Bollocks,' he said calmly.

'It is not bollocks. I saw that look on your face. You were going to beat him up.'

'What did you want me to do?'

'I wanted you to talk to him, for once in your life!'

'Talking to him won't do any good, for Christ's sake! He's way beyond that now! We've got to find some other way of keeping him away from Sefton or by Christ we'll end up visiting him in prison for the rest of our lives! And if that means giving him the odd hammering, then I'll certainly do that!'

Angie started to throw back a remark about Sefton but she only managed a few words before the tears welled up in her and she put her hand to her forehead to hide her eyes.

'Ah, for God's sake!' Stevie snapped. He snatched up his stick and hurried over to the door, slamming it hard behind him.

He poured himself a bowl of cornflakes and ate them in silence while Angie pottered around him in the kitchen, saying nothing in a meaningful way. At last he could take it no longer and he smacked his hand down on the table-top.

'All right!' he demanded harshly. 'What is it?'

'What do you mean, what is it?' Angie snapped back. 'Our only son is somewhere out there wandering around and all you can say is "What is it?" What sort of attitude is that! Some father you are!'

'Aw, for Jesus' sake, don't you start on me, as well!'

'You've done nothing but torture that boy for the last few weeks! You never leave off him! All you ever do is clump around the house moaning and whinging, and then when he comes home all you can do is shout at him!' Her face was red now and she was crying through her anger. 'It's no bloody wonder he's run away, and I'd be surprised if he ever comes back!' She let the tears flow then, dropping her head and hanging over the sink, sobbing into the palms of her hands. Stevie looked at her for a second, not knowing what to do, thinking that maybe he should go over to her and hold her. Then he stood up suddenly and went out into the hall.

'Fuck this,' he called to her. 'I'm going out for a walk.'

They met Hutchy at lunchtime, down by the harbour. The day was fresh and dry, but cold, and above the straight horizon of the sea was clear and blue.

'What happened to you?' he asked Colin, taking in the dishevelled clothes and the untidy hair.

'Long story.'

'Oh, aye? Fighting with your da again, were you?'

'Never mind,' Sefton said, intervening like a schoolteacher. 'Let's walk out to the end of the wall.'

The town harbour had originally been formed by the rocky promontory which jutted out in a dog leg from the top end of the promenade to form a small natural basin where a few fishing boats could ride safely at anchor. In the nineteenth century another, larger wall was built, hooking out and almost meeting the first, so that the only entrance to the harbour was the narrow gap between the two walls. Over the years the walls had been raised and improved, until now they were tall concrete affairs with a small beacon on each side of the gap. Sefton strolled out along the inner edge of the wall, stopping now and again to peer down into the few boats bobbing by its side.

'Dirty places, harbours,' he commented, nodding at the flotsam of empty plastic containers and cigarette ends lying on the oily water.

'So what's happening?' Hutchy asked.

190

'We're going to mount our first operation,' Sefton replied.

'About time.'

'What we have to decide is, who is going to be the first . . . target.'

'Oh.'

They walked out to where the beacon stood on its small red and white tower. People sometimes fished off the end of the wall but today it was empty. Sefton went up the few steps to the top of the wall and stood for a moment, staring out at the sea, watching the seagulls hanging immobile in the stiff breeze.

'Who, then?' Hutchy called up.

'Well, I've given it a lot of thought,' Sefton said quietly. 'It wasn't an easy task. I asked the Lord for guidance.'

'And what did he say?'

Sefton glared down at Hutchy, who smiled up at him. 'A joke,' Hutchy said, 'Just a joke.'

'He didn't say anything, Hutchy, he doesn't work that way. He gave me strength to help me make the decision. He came to me in the dark hours of the night and He gave me a staff to lean on. He eased my way.'

'So?' Hutchy asked. 'Who's it going to be?'

'It's going to be the manager at the golf club.'

Colin thought he hadn't heard right. 'You mean Barry Kelly?' he asked. 'From the golf club?'

'Yes.'

'No. You're pulling my leg, aren't you?'

'I'm deadly serious, Colin.'

'But he's not a terrorist!'

'He supplies information to terrorists. It's the same thing.'

'Who says he supplies information?'

'The police do, for one. They're sure he had something to do with the Mullan killing. How many times have you seen them going out to talk to him at the club?'

'He wasn't in those photographs!'

'This is recent intelligence, Colin. Extremely up to date.'

'Look, he's a nice bloke! He's been very good to me! He's been good to everyone in there.'

Sefton descended from the top of the wall and put his arm around Colin's shoulders. 'The devil comes in many guises, Colin. He hides his face. He doesn't show his true self. Ask yourself why Kelly was so good to everyone. Ask yourself why he got on with everyone. He had to become accepted, so that he could pass information back. That's the way these people work, Colin.'

It was all very plausible but it just didn't sound right. Colin eased himself free from the older man's arm. 'I don't mind being the executioner,' he said. 'I'm just not mad about being judge and jury, too.'

'It's the way it has to be. The police can't get enough evidence together to make a decent case. They can't do anything. So what does that mean, does that mean we leave him in place, scheming against our people, gathering information? Colin, someone told the IRA that Mullan played golf every Saturday morning. Someone passed the information. And to me, that's even worse than pulling the trigger because it's cowardly and underhand. It's up to us to do something about it. We're the only ones who can.'

Colin half expected him to say, 'Let us pray'. He thought about Kelly and how decent he had been.

He had truly seemed a nice person. And yet if what Sefton said was true, if he was passing information he would want to seem as friendly as possible. Images of the murder flew into his mind. The blood in the cap. The mess on the car.

Hutchy sniffed and rubbed at his nose. 'He's a Fenian, anyway,' he said. 'No great loss.'

'No,' said Colin after a moment. 'No, count me out on this one.'

'What do you mean, count you out?' Sefton asked.

'I don't want to be involved in this one. Not Kelly.'

Sefton stared at him for a long moment. 'We all have to do things we don't relish, Colin. That's a part of life.'

'I don't want to be involved in this. Anyone else. Not Kelly.' He reached out and toyed with a corroded steel ring set into the wall. Sefton rubbed at his chin. Hutchy smiled down at the oily water.

'Colin,' Sefton began quietly, 'I'm afraid you're in, whether you like it or not. We're all in it together now.' The tone of his voice said, I expected something like this from you. 'Let me remind you that we've all handled those weapons. But if you cast your mind back, you were the only one to handle the Browning. Your finger-prints are all over it, and only yours. It wouldn't do to have it dropped in with the local RUC, now, would it?'

So that was how it would be. Sefton was a bastard but then he had always known that. In a war you had to have bastards, they were the only ones who would take on the dirty work. Colin walked away from them and stood on the very end of the wall, staring out towards the sea. The breeze was whipping white tops from the grey-green of the waves. Small white clouds were drifting in from the horizon. In the back of his mind there were flares of anger, plans, retaliations; kill Sefton, kill Hutchy. Push them into the water, turn them in to the cops. Little raging thoughts flew round in his head like scraps of paper caught in a whirlwind but it was all too late now and there was no way out. Whatever he did, Sefton would manage to drag him down too. He looked out at the sea and his mind emptied and the little thoughts slowed down and fell. He felt sadness drift across him and it was heavy, physically heavy, bending his shoulders, weighing him down. Let it happen, he thought, let it run. It was out of control now, anyway, and nothing really mattered.

'All right,' he said, turning round. 'I'm in.'

'Good man,' Sefton said.

'But let's do it as soon as we can.'

'Well, you're the man with the inside knowledge. You know his routine. When can we do it?'

'Tomorrow,' Colin said. 'We can do it tomorrow.'

Barry heard the phone ringing from the bar and he hurried into his office to answer it, banging his knee painfully on the corner of the desk. 'Hello?' he asked, wincing and rubbing his leg.

'Mr Kelly. It's Colin Rea.'

'Oh, Colin. Hello.'

'Look, I've come down with some kind of bug. My mother says it's the flu. But I feel really terrible. Throwing up, and all, you know?'

'I know what you mean, Colin, there's a wee bug going around at the minute. Sure Joey Armstrong out of the kitchen has come down with it, too.'

'I'm not really well enough to come in tonight – '

'You're certainly not to come anywhere near this place until you're completely over it, do you hear me? You get to your bed. And drink plenty of water, that always helps. Have you got a temperature?'

'Ah . . . yes.'

'Aye. Well, look, come back in when you're feeling better. I'll get the others to cover for you.'

'Thanks, Mr Kelly.'

'That's all right. Get well soon.'

'Bye.' Colin set the phone down gently on the cradle. Sefton had put a Jesus Saves sticker on the centre of the dial, and had later coloured in the spaces in the letters with a biro. He looked down at the sticker for a long time and felt like Judas must have done after that last and fatal kiss.

They went out that afternoon in Sefton's car and drove to the golf club. Sefton slowed down as they passed the gates, and the three of them peered down the driveway.

'Long way to the clubhouse,' Hutchy remarked. He was sitting in the front seat beside Sefton.

'Not from where we're going to park,' Colin said.

Half a mile further on there was a narrow entrance where the wall around the club ended and a tall hedge began.

'Turn left here,' he said.

'Where does this go to?' Sefton asked.

'It leads up to the back gates of the club, but no one ever uses it.'

'What about deliveries, that sort of thing?'

'They all use the front gates. This road isn't marked as leading into the club.'

Half a mile down the narrow lane there was a widening of the road, and tall sycamore trees loomed above the grey stone wall.

'You can turn here,' Colin said.

They would leave the car here in the morning; it was only a hundred and fifty metres to the car park behind the clubhouse from the trees, and it wouldn't take long to run that. The plan had almost sprung into his head, and he had told them of it immediately. It was only later that he realised it was the same escape route that Mullan's killer had used. Now there's poetic justice for you, he had thought. He had no real stomach for the planning but he thought it would be all right on the day; that was why he wanted to do it as quickly as possible, to get it over with. If he waited too long, he thought he might come back to his senses.

'What about that wall?' Hutchy asked suspiciously.

'What about it?'

'Is it hard to get over?'

'I don't know, I've never tried it.'

'Go and try it, Hutchy,' Sefton directed.

'Why me?'

'You thought of it, you test it. Hurry up.'

He slammed the car door hard and jogged over to the wall. It was about chest height but he seemed to get over it easily enough. He came back brushing particles of moss from the front of his parka. 'No problem,' he said, swinging into the car again.

'Right,' Sefton said. 'From here we'll drive to the forest, and change cars. Let's see how long that takes.'

Twelve minutes later they were standing around the car in the centre of the same clearing they had used before. Nothing had changed. The trees still watched silently. The piles of rubbish still littered the verges. Perhaps it was colder.

'That should be all right,' Sefton said.

'Yeah,' said Hutchy. 'It'll take at least five minutes for

the first police car to make the golf club. We'll be well away by then.'

'What about the car?'

'That's your job, tonight.'

'No problem,' Hutchy replied happily.

It's like a dream, Colin thought, it isn't real. He felt detached and separate, as though all the trees and grass and mud and dirt were just backdrops on a film set. He was on the edge of things, and drifting.

On the drive back into town Sefton talked at great length about future 'operations'; Hutchy was staring straight out of the windscreen and might have been listening or might not, but Colin lay quietly in the back seat and thought about Mullan. They way they had argued that night in the car park, Mullan trying to warn him off. Don't throw it all away, he had said. He was a good strong man and now he was dead and the thought of it brought a stinging pain to his eyes. He wouldn't have liked this, Colin thought sadly, he wouldn't have liked this at all. But Mullan was dead and maybe Sefton was right, maybe someone should strike back, when the police and army weren't able to, or the thing would go on for ever. Someone had to act. As he stared out at the rolling, windswept farmland he wished he could talk it over with his father. Stevie would give good advice. But Stevie wouldn't listen, any mention of Sefton would no doubt lead to another digging session. It was up to Colin alone to make the decision. It was the first really big decision of his life and he wished there was someone he could share it with. Fuck it, he thought. There wasn't any choice anyway because he was well and truly stuck, Sefton had caught him with the fingerprints on the pistol and he was stuck with the pair of them, whatever happened.

'Are you sure he always goes out to the professional's shop at the same time every morning?' Sefton was asking.

'Yes. Always the same time.'

'Wouldn't do to be hanging around for too long, you know, waiting for him.'

'No, he's very punctual. He checks on the shop, then he opens the main bar.'

'I think it's best to do it in the open.'

'Easier to get away,' Hutchy added.

'Yes. But in case he runs. If he runs inside he could lock doors, couldn't he?'

'If he went into his office, there's a lock on that door,' Colin said.

'We couldn't get at him then, if he was locked in his office. It has to be done outside.'

'Who's going to do it, Sefton?' Hutchy was asking.

'I'm not sure.'

'I'll do it.'

'No.'

'Why not?'

'Colin will do it.'

Colin heard the words and his stomach chilled. 'Why me?' he asked.

'You're the best man for the job,' Sefton said.

'He'll screw it up!' Hutchy protested. 'I could do a far better job. Let me do it!'

Sefton shook his head slowly and didn't even look round at him. 'Colin will do it,' he said. 'He can take the Browning. You'll be a lookout, Hutchy, and you'll take one of the machine-guns.'

'He'll balls it up!'

'That's enough, Hutchy!'

Eventually the car pulled up outside Sefton's house and the neat row of pebble-dashed bungalows looked so normal and ordinary and there were seagulls cawing in the air as they got out. It was four o'clock and the sun was already low in the sky and Colin had a strange sense of the day drawing to a close. Night was coming and there was not a thing he could do to stop it. Tomorrow I will kill a man, he thought. Earlier the thought had made him sick in the stomach but he was numb to it now. Sefton slapped him on the back.

'Well, Colin,' he said cheerfully. 'I'll see you tomorrow, then.'

'Why me, Sefton? Why not Hutchy?'

'You're the best man for the job, Colin,' Sefton said softly, so that Hutchy wouldn't hear. 'Hutchy thinks he's hard but he might give in at the last minute, might refuse to go through with it. You won't.'

'What makes you so sure?'

'I'm sure. Don't worry, you'll be doing everyone a favour. Striking a blow for your country.' He grinned widely and left his hand on Colin's back for just a second too long and the boy pulled himself free.

'I suppose,' he said eventually.

He walked into town with Hutchy and neither of them spoke for a while, as though both were awed by the enormity of their plans. By the time they reached the promenade all the cars had their headlights on.

'What do you think, Hutchy?' Colin asked at last. 'Do you think this is right?'

Hutchy shrugged. 'Aye,' he said easily.

'Are you sure, though?'

'Aye.'

'I'm not sure.'

'You saw them shooting Mullan.'

'Aye, but Kelly didn't do it.'

'Well. Someone must have set Mullan up. Must have been him.'

'All right, suppose we go ahead and kill Kelly. What good is that going to do? What's that going to change?'

'We'll be even then. Them and us.'

'But then they'll just go and kill someone else.'

'They'll just go out and kill someone else anyway,' Hutchy said. 'At least Kelly won't be targeting for them.'

'Still, doesn't feel right, does it?'

'Nah, suppose it doesn't.' Hutchy swung out his foot to kick an empty Coke can into the roadway. 'I know what you mean. Sefton's weird sometimes, so he is. But a lot of what he says is right enough. And he did get those guns.'

'But we're planning to *kill* somebody, Hutchy. I mean, that's serious. Really serious. If we do this tomorrow, that's it. There'll be no going back.'

Hutchy shrugged and grinned at the same time, his face cruel and ugly in the half-light. 'It's a dirty job, Colin boy,' he said cheerfully, 'but someone's got to do it!'

He walked home at ten o'clock and they were both in the kitchen, not waiting for him but standing around as if expecting him. Angie didn't know whether to be angry or happy and she stood by the sink with her arms folded, struggling with herself. Colin felt a sudden stab of guilt at the pain he was undoubtedly causing her, pain that was written all across her face. Stevie was sitting at the kitchen table with the evening paper spread out in front of him.

'You're home, then,' he said slowly.

'I'm going up to the room,' Colin said, half-turning.

'You take one more step and I'll break your fucking leg.'

He turned back to face his father. 'What is it now?'

'Have a seat. We need to talk.'

'I don't think so.'

'Well I do. Sit down.'

There was a warning in his voice and Colin heeded it and sat down. It was all so tedious but if they wanted to bawl him out he might as well let them do it. After tomorrow it wouldn't matter anyway.

'Where were you all night?' Stevie asked.

'Out.'

'Your mother was worried about you. So was I.'

'I was all right.'

'So where were you?'

'Out. I told you. I was out.'

Stevie sighed, leaned back in the chair. 'Look, Colin. I'll be straight with you. I think you're getting into something you shouldn't, and I think that fellow Sefton has something to do with it. Now, you're a big lad, and you've got your own life to lead, I know that. But you need to be careful, too. And I don't want to lecture you, but I've made as many mistakes as a man could make, and if I'm to be of any use in this world, the least

I can do is pass that experience on to you. But you have to listen.'

'There's no need to worry, Dad,' Colin replied, but even as he said it he knew how hollow it sounded.

'Well, I think there is. And Mullan thought there was. Enough to give you a clip round the head.'

'Mullan is dead.'

'I know.' The old man ran his hand through his hair, frustrated and confused. Words were not his strong point. You couldn't beat words into someone's head.

'Sefton is . . . ah . . . well, I've met his kind before. They're . . . they use people. People like you. Young fellows. They twist them round and they send them out while they stay safely at home, with their hands clean. I've seen them before. And Sefton will use you, and young Hutchy, you mark my words!'

He paused, staring Colin in the eyes. Colin thought, I would have been angry last night, if he had come out with all this. Now I just don't care.

'Can I go now?' he asked politely. Stevie banged his hand on the table-top suddenly with a massive crack.

'No, you can't go! You can sit there until you've told us where you've bloody well been all night and all day!'

'I'm sorry,' Colin said, getting up. 'I've got to – '

'Get your backside back on that seat!'

'Don't give me any more orders, da,' Colin warned.

'I'll give you as many orders as I like,' Stevie growled, rising to his feet and lumbering round the table. He was frightening when he was angry, even with the stick clattering over the lino; it was as though he could take his entire bulk and direct every part of it into violence. It was like a tank lumbering round the table. 'You're still my bloody son and as long as you're living in this house you'll not give me any bloody cheek – '

Colin hadn't thought he was close enough to strike but suddenly his arm flicked out and caught Colin on the side of the face, open-handed. The force of the blow knocked him sideways and he fell against the kitchen units.

'No, Stevie!' Angie shrieked, running round the kitchen and grasping at his arm. 'Don't hit him!' Stevie shrugged her off and advanced towards his son.

Colin shook his head and it was as if all the numbness had cleared to leave only bright, glittering anger. He scrabbled to one side and jumped up.

'Don't you fucking well touch me again!' he shouted at the top of his voice. 'Don't you fucking touch me!'

'You're my bloody son – '

'Who the fuck are you to tell me what to do! Answer me that? Who are you to tell anybody what to do? I remember you, all right, I remember you, bringing those guns into the house years ago. You were up to your eyes in it, so you were! You have no right to preach!'

'Aye!' Stevie roared back. 'I was up to my eyes in it! You're right! I was a big man! Big Stevie! And look at me now, I'm nothing but a cripple who can't sleep at night! There's things I've done, son, that still come back to me in nightmares! Ten years later, and I still can't get away from it!'

His voice choked for a moment and Colin thought he would cry, but he swallowed and recovered his rage. He stabbed a forefinger towards Colin as he went on. 'I don't know what you and your friend Sefton are planning but just let me tell you this, as one who's been there: I hope you're able to live with yourself afterwards, that's all! I hope you can sleep at night!'

Colin felt himself near to crying with the frustration of it and the old man's eyes were filling too, and Angie was coming over and draping her arm around his shoulders, the tears streaming down her face.

'What did you do, then?' he asked, trying not to sob. 'What was it you fucking well did?'

'Forget it!'

'But I want to know!'

'It's none of your bloody business!'

'It is, it is my business! You're my bloody father! And the one time in my life when I might need a wee bit of help, you're too fucking wired-up to give it!'

Stevie grabbed for him again but he dodged it and ran to the door, fumbling with the handle, wanting only to get out of that kitchen and away from the tearful bloody faces and into somewhere quiet where he could weep and sob in peace.

He stayed in his room all night and fiddled with the guitar and listened to them arguing and fighting downstairs. He wanted someone to come up to see him. Either of them, it didn't matter who. If someone came up he would blurt it all out and that would be it over and the weight would have gone. Ah, Jesus, he thought, this is the rest of my life I'm going to fuck up. He picked at the guitar but none of the chords sounded right and the riffs were taut and jerky.

At about eleven o'clock their voices were even louder than normal, his mother shrieking at Stevie and Stevie roaring back, following each other from the living room to the kitchen and back to the living room. Colin listened silently with the tears dried on his cheeks. She's like a terrier, he thought, once she gets going, she never lets go. Shortly after that he heard the front door slamming, really hard, and his mother crying in the street. She would go round to one of the neighbours, probably, he thought, and cry on their shoulders.

He lay on the top of the bed and turned off the light and felt as sad as he had ever felt. It was like being alone in the middle of a vast, desolate landscape, where everything was burnt and ruined but you didn't know why. His mother might have come up to see him but Stevie never would, and so it was all finished. In the morning he would kill a man he liked and it would be all finished.

It helped to pull back into his mind the images of Mullan dying. The man who had been his friend, if he had only known. The cap, filling with blood. When he thought about that and about the man who had done it the anger came back and his heart hardened. Probably everyone had to do that, remember all the bad things before shooting someone. Stoke up the hatred. Throw petrol on it, so that it whooshed skywards, incinerating. Even though it was necessary and had to be done, you needed to have anger to actually do it, to actually pull the trigger. I'll have anger, he thought. By God, I'll have lots of anger.

The pale yellow streetlight was coming through the patterned curtains and he let his eyes follow the angular design, dark and light rectangles interesecting each other, down one side and up the other. The curtains had been there for years, since he was at school. When he

was ill and stayed in bed with the flu he had stared up
at the same curtains, framing their rectangle of even
grey sky, measuring with his eyes the same pattern. I
never thought I would come to this, he thought, never
in my wildest dreams. Or nightmares.

The next morning was clear and bright and there were seagulls flying around outside the house, cawing at each other. It had to be a nice day, Colin thought sourly, lying immobile in bed and staring at the ceiling. Why couldn't it have rained?

He dressed carefully, thinking that the clothes he put on would see him through a momentous day in his life. I'll become a murderer today. Better look my best. He wore his good jeans and his old, raggy sweatshirt which always brought him luck. He cleaned his teeth for a long time, trying not to look at himself in the mirror.

By the time he came down to get breakfast his mother had left for work and he felt a pang of regret at not seeing her one more time before the deed. Stevie was sitting in his usual chair in the living room staring at the television and they ignored each other. He poured his usual bowl of Sugar Puffs and ate them slowly. It's like I'm saying goodbye to everything, he thought, I wonder why that is. I'll be back tonight, after all. Nothing will change. I'll still pour milk on these Sugar Puffs tomorrow. They'll still turn the milk a pale shade of brown. He'll still stare at the TV and mum'll still go off to work and nothing will change. Not really.

He put on his old, tatty combat jacket because it was warm and because it might be like combat, later on. He was on his way out of the back door when his father spoke for the first time.

'Where are you going?' he asked.

'Out.'

'Why not use the front door? Ashamed?'

'No . . . A change, that's all.'

'You remember what I told you, all right? Think about it.'

'Aye,' Colin replied lightly. 'Sure.' He stepped out through the back door and closed it gently behind him.

He arrived at Sefton's house at 9.23 exactly. Sefton was waiting in the front room, nervous.

'Hutchy isn't here yet. He said he'd be here by nine.'

'He'll be here,' Colin said. 'There's plenty of time.'

'I hope so.'

Sefton was probably imagining that Hutchy had been arrested stealing the car, or something. It didn't matter to Colin now, for some reason. It was a beautiful, clear, winter day and the hard blue sky reached from horizon to horizon and the seagulls had been wheeling round the harbour as he walked by. You couldn't ask for more.

They had decided that if they weren't at the golf club by ten o'clock the thing would be called off; after that they couldn't be sure of getting Kelly in the open. Colin had prayed for something like this to happen, some unavoidable delay which wasn't his fault. It was odd, but now that there was a chance of postponing the killing, or even cancelling it, he felt nothing. Nothing at all. As if his feelings had all been sluiced out and he was just a hollow shell.

Hutchy arrived at 9.40, driving a big new shiny Ford Sierra. He pulled up at the kerb and hooted the horn. Sefton grimaced.

'I told him not to do that,' he said.

'What about the guns?' Colin asked.

'They're here. In the bag. I loaded the ammunition myself.'

'What about the masks?'

'They're in there too.'

'All right.'

They walked casually to the car. Sefton swinging the sports-bag in his hand. Hutchy leered out of the driver's side window.

'Well, Colin, boy,' he called. 'All ready to rock and roll?'

'Don't you worry, Hutchy,' Colin replied. 'Don't you worry about a thing.'

Sefton got into his own car and Colin joined Hutchy in the stolen Sierra. They would drive to the forest and leave Sefton's car there, going on to the golf club in the Sierra. After the shooting they would leave the Sierra in the clearing, burned out, and drive home in Sefton's Volvo. Funny expression, that, Colin reflected. To drive home after a killing. How can you 'drive home' after something like that?

Sefton pulled his Volvo out into the road and Hutchy

moved off after him, carefully, keeping the speed down to avoid the police. The last thing they wanted was to be stopped for speeding in a stolen car.

'I wanted to do this, you know,' Hutchy said.

'I know,' Colin replied.

'Sefton's only letting you do it to make sure you're in, you know that, don't you?'

'Yeah.'

'I'm doing the next one, though.'

'If you like.'

They drove on in silence for a while. Then Hutchy asked, 'Are you still worried about all this?'

'Yeah.'

'I was thinking about it last night, so I was. About what Sefton said and all. And what you said, too.'

'So what did you decide?'

'Has to be done,' he said seriously. 'It's not very nice, but it has to be done. I mean, they never gave Mullan a chance, did they?'

'Well. In an hour's time it'll not matter. It'll be done and finished with.'

'I've never seen anybody getting killed.'

'You're not missing much.'

They made the forest by 9.51. Sefton pulled his car up as close to the trees as he could get it, and Hutchy bounced the Sierra round to face down the narrow track again, pulling to a halt beside the old Volvo. Sefton hurried across with the sports-bag.

'We're late,' he said, throwing himself into the back seat.

'Relax, would you,' Colin said. 'We've plenty of time.

He doesn't actually go to the professional's shop until half-ten. We've loads of time.'

'Well we don't want to waste it. Here.' He held out the Browning to Colin. 'You take that one. Hutchy, here's the machine-gun for you. You're the lookout. I loaded them.'

Colin hefted the pistol in his hand. It felt heavier with a full magazine of bullets, butt-heavy, and there was a tightness about it which made his heart pump. It felt small and hard and dangerous. A thought flashed across his mind like ticker-tape, I could kill the two of them now, I could kill the two of them now. He slid out the magazine and looked at the round in the feed lips. It was dull and brassy, with a round copper head, and he ran the pad of his thumb lovingly over the smoothness of it. 'How many rounds?' he asked.

'Twelve. If you can't hit him with twelve rounds then we've been wasting our time.'

'Sefton, stay calm.'

'I am calm.'

Hutchy opened the stock of the machine-gun and pulled out the magazine and looked at it, too. He grunted. 'They even look dangerous, don't they?'

'Look, we need to move here,' Sefton said, peering nervously through the side windows. 'We must keep to the timings.'

'Okay,' Hutchy said. He slapped the magazine back into the weapon and pushed it carefully underneath the driver's seat. 'I'll be watching your back, Colin,' he grinned. 'God help anyone comes near me.'

They bumped out on to the road again and turned towards the club. Colin wondered what Barry Kelly would be doing at that point, what he would be thinking about. They should really have warned him first, he reflected, so that he could make his peace with God. Catholics were funny about that sort of thing, apparently. He could have spent an hour or two in confession, or whatever it was they did. He wouldn't be aware that this was his last hour on earth, for ever. Poor sod.

At that precise moment Barry Kelly was sitting on the side of his bed, half-dressed, holding a mug of luke-warm coffee in his lap, staring at the wall in front of him. He sat immobile for a long time and then slowly raised his left hand and glanced at his watch. He was late. He had always made a point of getting out of bed in time and being punctual in the mornings but today he was late. This is the start of it, he thought sadly, this is the top of the slippery slope, and it's a long way down.

He rubbed tenderly at his lower lip, feeling around the area where McKay's punch had landed on him. McKay was a bastard. If they were going to shoot anyone, they should have killed McKay. There had been no call for that, no call for it at all, and especially not in front of the whole lounge.

Of course the man had been drinking heavily earlier in the evening and maybe all day, judging by the way he had staggered into the lounge. And he was big enough to be frightening, big enough so that the men standing around the bar eased off to each side, giving him room. Ernie had noticed him first and had nudged Barry and nodded at the big man, staring down at the whiskey tumbler on the counter. 'Watch out for him,' he had whispered.

And then it had begun, the snide remarks under his breath every time Barry had moved past him, Fenian, taig, Provie. Of course the only thing to do was ignore him and hope he went peacefully away. Barry had long since learned not to argue with a drunk; but when McKay had snatched up the glass and hurled it across the bar at him, that was when he had to draw the line. It was amazing how the low drone of conversation died so suddenly into silence, leaving the two of them facing each other across the bar, the giant drunk and the chubby bar manager, one pissed and the other terrified.

He looked around the room at the clothes strewn across the furniture and thought again about getting up. There was a throbbing ache under his armpit and he was worried in case McKay had broken one of his ribs when he had started kicking him; there was a brief stab of pain every time he took a breath and he had read somewhere that that was a sign of a broken rib. It wasn't pleasant to think of a bone, broken. I don't mind the odd swollen lip or blacked eye, he thought, but broken bones were something he didn't like to think about.

The worst thing was that no one had tried to help. No one had rushed forward to pull McKay off him, to hold him back, and all right, McKay was a big lad but there were twenty-odd people there and they could have held him. But instead they watched, shocked and curious, keeping well back for safety but still close enough to see. They knew this fight wouldn't spread. They knew that McKay was only after one person. Maybe he did do it, they were thinking. Maybe McKay was right, after all. Barry knew that most of them had no time for McKay, but even animals can be right, sometimes, and that was how they would think, that was how they would work it out. He may be a drunken bastard, they would think, but at least he's one of us.

He should never have left the safety of the bar. Once round the corner and into the lounge he had been easy meat and after all, he was a manager, not a tag wrestler. But he was a reasonable man and he generally expected reasonable behaviour from others; that was his weakness, really, and so the first, sudden punch had come as such a surprise. And the tumbling over on to the floor and the steely taste of blood round his teeth, and the thudding impacts of the boots hitting the body. So much for reason, he had thought, curling up into a ball and hoping to survive. Ah, well. At least there were no teeth missing. He looked down at the cold coffee swilling around in the cup. Time to get up, he thought.

He went downstairs to his office and unlocked the desk and pulled out a single sheet of paper, typed on the old club machine with the falling 'a'. He had started to type it the previous evening and had got as far as 'that I can no longer work in this position . . .' before the words had all dried up. He didn't want to resign. There were very few jobs to be had, but at the same time he didn't want to spend the next two years getting beaten up by every drunken bigot who wanted to take it out on a Fenian. You could take so much, but only so much, and then you had to do something. And he wasn't a fighter. Maybe they realised that, he thought, maybe that's why they're picking on me. Because they know I won't fight back.

He stood by the desk for a long while, staring down at the half-finished letter, then with a sudden impatient gesture he crumpled it into a ball and tossed it into the waste-paper basket. To hell with them, he thought. They won't put me out. He slammed the drawer shut and locked it again. To hell with them. It was only a little rebellion but it was enough, and he felt a quick surge of pride. There wasn't much in his life to be proud of, really; a broken marriage, a lot of dead-end jobs. He would stick this one out. He would make this one work, no matter what. Screw them and their bigotry.

He glanced at his watch and it was ten twenty-five and he was due to make his normal visit to the professional's shop. Right, he thought. Back to normal. No more of this dozing around. Fight back. Screw them.

He strode down the narrow corridor to the back door and pulled it open, walking briskly out into the fresh morning air, inhaling deeply as the sharp cold nipped at him. The freshness of it made him feel a little better. It was a beautiful day. A seagull had perched itself on top of the old stables building and it was brilliant white against the sky and its beak was a raw, natural orange colour, and as he watched it cawed arrogantly at him. As he started across the yard a tractor gurgled into life somewhere near the groundsman's huts and the sound seemed to reverberate and echo through the still, bright day. A good day to be alive, he thought, filling his lungs with the cold winter air.

Colin walked steadily across the car park, breathing deeply, fighting down an overwhelming urge to run. Sefton had told him to walk because a running man draws the attention but it was easier said than done. The pistol was pulling down his right jacket pocket and banging off his thigh as he walked, and the black mask with the eyeholes was bulging in his left. Every few steps he patted each one to reassure himself. The car-park seemed a mile wide. There were a lot of cars there and the sunlight glinted on wing-mirrors and wind-screens, blinding him. He was excited and frightened and sad and angry all at the same time, a mad turmoil of emotions. I wish this was over, he thought. I wish it was done. I've never felt my heart beat like this before.

He kept his eyes fixed on the dark grey bulk of the clubhouse ahead of him, watching the doors and win-dows, waiting for movement. The building was familiar and yet strangely unreal, as though it were some sort of model with a few details changed. A film set. I'll get to the clubhouse and it'll just be a front, he thought, nothing round the back but framework and props, and there'll be cameras and lights and the whole film crew there waiting. Some hope.

He reached the steps at the end of the car-park and took them three at a time, moving on to the drive and across to the back wall of the stables. His feet crun-ched on the gravel, painfully loud. The old stables were now the locker rooms but there were no back windows and he could stop there to slip on the mask. And cock the gun, remember to cock the gun. He ran the last few steps and hit the wall hard with his back, pressing tight against it, looking straight down at the tenth fairway but there was no one on it. Off to the right were the trees and behind them Hutchy and Sefton were in the car, waiting to hear the shots.

He put his hand into the jacket pocket and grasped the mask and then hesitated because once the mask was on there was no going back, definitely no going back. He could explain his presence there as long as no one searched him, but not with a mask on. A mask was guilt, and it was ready in his pocket. Look, it's simple, he told himself, all I have to do is walk through the courtyard and find Kelly and shoot him, boom-boom then run, that's all, only take a second. He dragged images of Mullan's death back into his mind to try and raise the anger; the blood, the cap, the tiny pieces of clean white bone stuck to the inside of the hatchback. They killed him. He didn't deserve it. Kelly deserves it. But no matter how hard he remembered the anger wouldn't come and the longer he waited the more nervous he became. After a few seconds he took a deep breath and tugged the mask from his pocket and pulled it quickly down over his head, adjusting the eyeholes so that he could see properly. The coarse wool prickled the hot, sweaty skin on his face and there was no hole for his nose so he breathed through his mouth, listening to the quick rise and fall of it. That's done it now, he thought. He slid his hand into the other pocket and curled his fingers around the grip of the pistol. He wanted to stay there, he wanted to wait, think it over, maybe change his mind. Maybe this isn't the way. Maybe there's another way. He put his hand to the mask, grasped it, then hesitated again. What do I do, he thought frantically, for God's sake, what do I do?

At that moment the tractor by the groundsman's huts burst into life and the suddenness of the noise made him jump, adrenalin burning through his system. He was moving before he realised, pushing off from the wall and walking quickly out on to the gravel drive. He was moving like a sleepwalker, hardly aware of what he was doing, his vision tunnelled into one area of interest, nothing to left or right, only what was ahead. Sweat tickled beneath the mask. He walked through the archway and into the courtyard and there he was, right in the middle, Kelly, his face white and his eyes wide and staring. He sees the mask, Colin thought, he sees only the mask and that is terror on his face.

Kelly was frozen in the centre of the courtyard, his hands still in his pockets, his shoulders hunched, his mouth hanging open. Suddenly Colin felt the hatred flash from nowhere into his heart and he tugged out the gun and pointed it at Kelly, holding it in both hands. Kelly began to shake his head, slowly at first, then faster, pulling his hands from his pockets and pushing them out to him, palms first, pleading, and Colin centred the foresight on his chest and squeezed the trigger as gently as he could, tensing himself for the bang. Nothing. He squeezed harder, once, twice, and still nothing, and then he remembered that he hadn't cocked the thing but Kelly had noticed and he was already starting to move, turning and heading for the back door of the clubhouse.

It seemed that time had slowed down in some way; each second was suddenly taking minutes to elapse and there seemed to be a vastness of time for everything to happen in. Now all his thoughts were cool, calm, existing in their own proof of separation, thoughts appearing in his mind and slipping into action with no conscious decision. He pulled back the slide and cocked the pistol and aimed it again but by this time Kelly was almost at

219

the door and diving through it even as he watched. Colin began to jog after him. There was no panic, no fear, only the purpose burning in his head. You're not getting away from me, you bastard. Through the familiar back door and Kelly had fallen over the doorstep but was just getting up again and he snatched the pistol up but the other man was too quick, cannoning off the wall and diving through into the main lounge. Colin swore. He didn't want to go too far into the building but he didn't want Kelly to get away, not now, not once the thing was started. He owed someone a death and he was damn well going to deliver.

He moved slowly down the corridor and into the lounge and there he was, over at the window, scrabbling at a catch and Colin thought, how in the hell would you ever get out of there, anyway? Kelly looked round over his shoulder and his body tensed suddenly, as though he realised that he was finished now, that his life was about to end. He pushed back hard against the padded upholstery, his head jerking and shaking and a dark stain appearing round his crotch, growing bigger. Dirty bastard, Colin thought, advancing on him, raising the pistol to the aim. Dirty Fenian bastard, pissing yourself like that. Sefton was right. People like you don't deserve to live.

He centred the foresight again on the chest and took up the first pressure on the trigger and then Kelly spoke, for the first time, a tiny, frightened, gurgling voice.

'Please don't shoot me,' he said simply. 'Dear God, please don't shoot me. I don't want to die.'

Later, when he thought about it, he compared the sensation to a drenching with ice-cold water, poured over him all at once. All of a sudden Kelly was no longer a Provie or a Fenian or a taig or any other kind of label but just a simple, frightened ordinary man who didn't want his life to end and was pissing his trousers from uncontrollable fear. After all the stories and speeches and politics and words it all came down to this, a scared, defenceless man who had pissed himself and expected to die. It was the lowest thing he had ever seen. There is no honour in this, Colin thought, there is no honour. This will not honour any memory.

Kelly was crying openly now, his face red and twisted like a child's, his eyes screwed up tight as though expecting a blow. He had clasped both his hands across the damp patch in his trousers as though trying to preserve some dignity in his final desperate moments of life. Colin felt sickened and ashamed, embarrassed by the mask and the gun in his hand. For the first time in his life he honestly loathed himself and the thing he had become.

Suddenly it was too much to bear and he swung the pistol upwards and pulled the trigger, firing into the ceiling, the bang deafening him and the sudden jerk of the recoil almost tugging the weapon from his hand. The ejected case tinkled off one of the tables, and he pulled the trigger again and again, and then again a fourth time, shouting as he did so, a scream of pain and fear and anger lost in the massive crashing of the gun. The secret was that there was nothing to kill. He had come all this way to find that out, that there was nothing at the end but a shivering, whimpering, terrified man. Sefton didn't know that, neither did Hutchy, they thought it was war. This wasn't war. This was murder.

Kelly shouted and flinched at the first shot, rolling himself into a foetal ball with his hands opened out across his head and his fingers shaking. Colin wanted to talk to him, to tell him that it didn't matter, that he was all right, that the whole thing had been a mistake. But it was all gone far beyond talking now and he had to get away and then suddenly he was running, out of the lounge and along the narrow corridor to the court-yard, bursting out into the sunlight, tearing through the archway. There were pale faces staring out from the professional's shop window as he passed. Down the steps and through the car park, running as he had never run before, dodging and swerving around all the parked cars, sliding once and banging his shin on a bumper. The faster he ran the stronger his urge to flee became, until it was swelling in his chest like a burning balloon and all that mattered was to put distance between him-self and the poor, weeping bastard curled up in the lounge.

He hit the wall with a bump and threw himself over it, winding himself, the rough stone jarring in his chest. Hutchy was standing by the car, the sub-machine-gun dangling from his hand. He looked nervous.

'What happened?' he demanded. 'We didn't hear any shots.'

'Inside,' Colin panted, bent over.

'Inside the clubhouse?'

'Yes.'

Sefton emerged from the car, holding on to the open door. 'Did you get him?'

Colin straightened up and shook his head.

'Well, what happened, then?' Hutchy demanded again, louder this time.

'I didn't kill him.'

'You didn't kill him? Well, why not for fuck's sake?'

Colin shook his head, wanting to explain but panting too heavily. Hutchy looked round at Sefton. 'The fucker isn't dead,' he said.

'I know.' Sefton was pale and nervous, gnawing at his lower lip. 'We'd better go.'

'Fuck that,' Hutchy said, spitting harshly. He swung up the machine-gun and cocked it. 'I'll do it.'

'You can't do it, not now!' Sefton protested.

'It'll be a few minutes yet before the cops arrive. I'll have plenty of time.'

'No, Hutchy!' Sefton commanded, but his nerves had got the better of him and the words came out in a whimper. Hutchy was almost at the wall when Colin grabbed at his arm.

'No, Hutchy. Leave him,' he gasped.

'Get the fuck off me!' he snarled back, his eyes wild. He's snapped, Colin thought suddenly. He's cracked up. 'You couldn't kill him, let me go and finish the job!'

'You can't kill him!'

'Why not?'

'It's not right!'

Hutchy looked at Colin as though he had two heads, then shrugged him off and turned to the wall. Before he knew what he was doing Colin had grabbed him by the shoulder of his jacket and was spinning him round. There was no time to explain about how wrong it was and how it would change nothing and he would have to use force, but suddenly the barrel of the machine-gun whipped round and caught him on the chin in a jarring, ripping impact. He fell backwards, pain stabbing through his jaw.

'Get the fuck off me!' Hutchy roared, swinging the gun again. Colin jumped to one side, narrowly missing the barrel.

'We have to get out of here,' Sefton was pleading from the car. Hutchy was rushing towards Colin with all his weight behind the butt of the weapon and there was no time to swerve so Colin lowered his head and leaned in low and hard, his shoulder catching his friend in the stomach and the machine-gun cracking down on his shoulder. Hutchy blew all his breath out in a long whoof! and Colin could smell the sweat from his armpits as he pushed, trying to topple him over.

'For Christ's sake, we haven't got time for this!' Sefton shouted.

'Bastard!' Hutchy wheezed. Colin jabbed three or four times into the crotch and the big fellow grunted from the pain and dragged the gun down, between them, trying to use it as a lever. He was fighting mad now. Colin felt his strength beginning to ebb. The gun was between them, hard against Colin's cheek, and Hutchy was pushing it as hard as he could and he was very strong but then he lost his footing and they both fell, tangled together and still struggling. They landed hard on the damp grass by the wall and then there was the earsplitting crash of the gun going off and Colin felt the sharp flick of the air as the bullets passed within inches of his face. Hutchy screamed and released his grip, and Colin jumped backwards, rolling off and on to the grass.

224

'Oh, God!' Sefton was shouting. 'Oh dear God Jesus!'

The machine-gun had gone off when the muzzle was next to Hutchy's face and the bullets had carved a deep groove along his cheek from his lip to his eye, a thick flap of skin hanging free and exposing his teeth in a terrible, agonised grin. There was blood all over his face, trickling from the wound.

'Jesus,' Colin breathed. Hutchy had screamed once then stopped and now he was lying still, his eyes closed, the blood running down his neck and on to the wet grass. 'You've killed him,' Sefton said. 'We've got to get out of here!'

Colin looked up at him, then down again at the prone body of his friend, and then the hatred boiled in his chest again because Sefton had brought them to this, Sefton had talked them into it with his crap about wars and rights and honour. This was his war, not theirs. Bastard. Suddenly he remembered the pistol in his pocket and he grabbed for it, snagging the hammer on his pocket and having to wriggle about to free it. Sefton realised instantly what he was going to do and his mouth fell open for a second, then he threw himself into the car and slammed the door, making sure to push down the lock and Colin thought, 'That won't help you, you bastard.' He pulled out the gun and aimed it roughly at the car and snatched at the trigger, feeling it jerk in his hand with each shot. There was a distinct clunk as a bullet entered the metal of the car, then another, but then Sefton had pulled the car off and away, the engine revving madly and stones and dirt flying from the tyres. Colin pointed the pistol down the road after him and fired another useless shot, then the car was gone and the lane was empty and there was just himself and his friend and the empty ringing in his ears. And then he ran.

It seemed that he ran for hours, maddened, but with an animal's sense of shade and cover. He ran along hedges and through copses, scratching his face and hands on the low twigs, catching his feet on thorns. He fell many times, smearing mud and grass on the knees of his jeans, cutting his palms on small stones as he landed. He cut around farms and bungalows, avoided roads, keeping to the wild country. Several times he hid from helicopters, scrambling under hedges or pressing flat against walls. He passed several herds of cows staring stupidly at him as he trespassed across their fields.

There was no thought as he ran, no reflection, just the burning urge to escape, to get away, to reach that safe place where he could hide and clean himself. There was no thought because there was no safe place and the mind would not accept that. He focused on his flight, on staying upright, on the pain from his chin where the machine-gun had hit him.

At the top of the grassy hill he lay on the damp grass and watched as two army Landrovers pulled up on the road below, the soldiers getting wearily out of the vehicles and setting up their signs and bollards, taking up position in the ditches, stopping the first cars that came along. They were perhaps two hundred yards away but he held his breath all the same, frightened by the loudness of his panting. The soldiers would be looking for him. He was a murderer. A killer of a friend.

He ran again, heading for the sea, the pain of the

running pushing other thoughts from his mind. Near the coast there were more houses, farms and expensive bungalows, and he slowed down, walking quickly by the side of the narrow country roads. Without any conscious decision he found himself on the long twisting road which lead down to the dunes and he followed it, smelling the sea as he drew nearer. Along the side of the road there were bungalows where no one ever seemed to live, their doors always closed and their venetian blinds down, and he hurried past them, keeping his eyes straight ahead as though afraid to meet some dead blank gaze. There was a narrow path leading away from the road and a loose wire fence and then he was in the dunes, stumbling along the paths the children had made, paths he had made, in his time.

He headed for the centre of the dunes, for the big dune, where he couldn't be seen from the town or the beach, scrabbling up the steep slope and slamming down at last in the tall, coarse grass with his breath rasping in his throat and his legs and body aching. He lay back on the sand and stared up into the cold, blue sky, dragging air into his lungs, breathing.

He lay still for a long time, hours, perhaps. Time meant nothing to him. The tide was coming in and he could hear the surf coming on to the beach, rattling over the pebbles near the high tide mark, and seagulls wheeled and played above him, cawing to each other in their innocence. He gently moved each part of his body, feeling for pain or damage, wincing when he found it. His jaw was the worst, stinging painfully where the gun barrel had connected it; he touched gingerly at the wound and there was bright blood on his fingers. Other parts of his body ached too, from the run; his legs, his knees, the palms of his hands. His jeans were ripped at the right knee and he could feel dry, crusty blood on his leg.

There were wispy smears of clouds forming in the sky and he watched them for a while as they thickened and drew together and formed heavier clumps of white. He didn't want to think about anything, but he had to do something. He couldn't just lie there forever. But there was no way out, and no matter how he approached it the same fact flew up to the front of his mind; there was no way out. Hutchy was dead and they would find the body and identify it. They would find the machine-gun. Kelly would have reported the attempt on his life by now, and it would be obvious that Hutchy was involved in some way, and they would start to look for all his friends and associates. Himself. Sefton. They would call at the house and Stevie would let them in and they would tell him what had happened, and Stevie would know the truth of it right away. The old bastard was smart enough, you had to give him that, he'd put two and two together right away. Well, at least they'd pick up Sefton and maybe give him a kicking.

So he was done for, whatever way he looked at it. Fucked. Shafted. And it was all Sefton's fault. Colin remembered the way Kelly had huddled up into a ball in the lounge, with the urine stain spreading over his crotch, terrified. He hadn't felt like much of a hero then. It was just a foul, cruel business, to destroy a man like that, who couldn't fight back. There was no honour in that at all. Thank God I didn't kill him, he thought.

That's something, at least. It would be terrible to lie here and have that on my conscience too.

It was different with Hutchy; they had been fighting and Hutchy had been killed and somehow that was fair. He hadn't meant to do it and anyway it was Hutchy's fault for starting to fight; if he hadn't gone so completely buck-mad then he might still be alive. If they hadn't gone to Sefton's house that morning he might still be alive. If they hadn't ... he began to run back through his memory, searching out all the moments on which his destiny could now be seen to have pivoted, all the times he could have chosen another way. The time he walked out of the training session. The time he didn't use the confidential telephone. The time Mullan had slapped him in the car park. All moments when he could have turned and chosen another way, taken another path which might not have led to these dunes and this terrible, crushing sadness.

But then he hadn't chosen. He tried to think of any conscious decision he had made, choosing to go with Sefton and his plans, and could remember none. He had drifted along like deadwood on the tide, and now he was washed up and abandoned. He felt like weeping but it was hard to cry on your back. His eyes watered, though. Poor Hutchy, he thought, I wonder where he is now?

After a while he sat up and looked around him, trying to get his bearings. He was halfway along the strand and well back among the dunes; off to the right he could see the big dune, and beyond that the pale bulk of the convent sitting up on the low cliffs. Off to the left the dunes seemed to go on for miles. He sniffed. He could go home, he could walk along the beach and go back home and it would take about twenty-five minutes but they would be waiting there for him. He could walk the other way, along the mile and a half of beach to where the river Bann joined the sea, but the river was too wide to swim and even if he could swim it, there was nothing on the other side. He could make Donegal, hide out there. He had never been to Donegal, never been south of the border. To get there he would have to cross the Bann then walk to the Foyle and somehow get across that, or else go down through Derry and go that way but then the troops on the border would probably pick him up.

He was tying himself up in knots. To hell with it, he thought. I don't want to go to prison. He put his hand into his pocket and fingered the gun, still there after all his falls and tumbles. That was a way out but he didn't want to think about it too much. If there was someone who could do it for him when he wasn't looking or expecting it then that might be all right, but he didn't want to do it himself. He tried not to think about it for a while, but eventually he pulled the gun out of his pocket and looked at it as though it was something he had just picked out. The odour of gun-smoke was still hanging round it and he put it to his nose and sniffed it, the smell taking him suddenly back to the lounge and Kelly and the damp patch on the trousers. He slid out the magazine and unloaded all the cartridges and there were only three left. Surely to God it wouldn't take three shots. He loaded the magazine again and shoved it back into the butt of the weapon and then remembered that there would be another round in the chamber and so that was four. More than enough, he thought, more than enough.

He crawled forwards slightly until he could see the flat line of the sea, dark against the sky, just above the grassy crests of the dunes. There were clouds gathering out there on the horizon, big, woolly white clouds which seemed to be billowing out of the sea with infinite slowness. He would go to prison, without a doubt; ten years, probably, and maybe more. If he could prove that it was an accident, that he hadn't meant to kill Hutchy. But then, what would the judges care about him, he was just another young terrorist whose ways had found him out. He thought about prison, what it would be like to stay in the same room with the same people for years and years on end. Seven days a week, four weeks a month, twelve months a year. And for how many years? If he got ten years, he might get out when he was twenty-eight or so. That was his life gone. What could you do when you were twenty-eight, and had never done anything? He had never had a woman. The thought suddenly chilled him; what woman would look at him when he came out of prison? He felt the hot stinging tears welling up behind his eyes and he fought them down, not wanting to cry. I'm not a child any more, he told himself. I won't cry. All of a sudden losing his virginity had become of towering importance to him, and he wished he knew a girl, any girl, well enough to go to her and ask her help, ask her to let him do it to her just once before the end. There were some of the girls from school but he hadn't seen them for ages and they had mostly laughed at him anyhow.

He sat for a long time feeling very sorry for himself.

The breeze was strengthening, tugging at locks of his hair, chilling him. Eventually he shifted and moved forwards to a small ridge of sand at the back of the strand, settling on his stomach with his head behind the thick grass and just a big enough gap to see on to the beach. There was one car parked, on up towards the town, and a man and his dog were walking on the edge of the surf and there was no other activity. He wondered idly how long he could hide there before hunger drove him out to find food. Not long, probably.

He put his hand in his pocket and toyed with the pistol again. He suspected that the best way to do it would be in a swift rush, pulling the pistol out and putting it at his temple and pulling the trigger all in one smooth, rapid movement, and then it would be done before the body really knew about it. But what if he snatched the trigger and missed, or only wounded himself? What if, in those last frantic milliseconds between the pulling of the trigger and the impact of the bullet, as the bullet rushed up the barrel towards his head, what if he changed his mind? When there was nothing left to do but take the impact? And if he was wounded, and unable to move, what sort of death would that be? Lying there until the seagulls came for him. Agony. Hutchy had been lucky, at least it had been quick.

There was a figure on the beach and he watched it for at least ten minutes before something familiar about the movement caused him to look more closely. It was coming from the town end of the strand and moving quite slowly, but as it grew nearer Colin recognised the jerky, twisting movement and the broad, bulky shoulders and the stick held close in to his hip for support. It was Stevie, lumbering along near the top of the beach. Colin felt a sudden swoop of happiness, as if the sun had come out from behind clouds and shone briefly on him, but then he wondered what he would tell his father, and the sunshine disappeared. He had let the old man down. He had ignored all the warnings and the old bastard had been right after all. He was obviously out on one of his walks. Colin slid back down a little to keep out of sight, but staying where he could still peer through the dry grass stalks at the limping figure coming up the beach.

Stevie came up slowly, struggling in the soft sand, his stick occasionally sinking into it and causing him to lurch to one side. He would probably have found it easier further down on the firmer damp sand but for some reason he stayed near the dunes. He passed about thirty or forty yards from where Colin was hidden and walked on a short distance before stopping and leaning on his stick, as though tired. Then after a moment he straightened up and, putting his free hand to the small of his back, he shouted at the top of his voice.

'Colin!' he roared. It was a command, rather than a call. 'Colin! Where are you?'

Colin scrabbled backwards in panic, crawling out of sight. How had the old bastard found him? How did he know? More important, who had be brought with him? He lay still for a second, then crawled up to the crest again and peered through the grass at the far end of the beach. Nothing. The car was still there, but the man with the dog was at the far end now and mounting the rocks which lead to the town.

'Colin!'

He wanted to run down and talk to the old man but he was frightened and confused and couldn't work out how he had been discovered. It wasn't a trap because there was no one else with him. And he still had the gun. Anyway, what could the old fellow do out here?

Stevie had listened for a reply and, hearing none, had started to limp on down the beach again when Colin finally stood up and stepped awkwardly down the sandy slope on to the beach. Some sense caused the old man to stop, aware of the presence behind him. Colin stood loosely with the gun pulling down one side of his jacket, not sure why he had moved. Stevie turned round slowly, using the stick for support, until he was facing his son across thirty yards of sand. The wind caught a strand of his hair and pulled it upright. God, he looks tired, Colin thought.

'Well,' Stevie called out, the breeze making his voice ragged. 'You've really got yourself in the shit this time, haven't you?'

'How did you know where to find me?'

'Where else would you bloody well go? You used to spend all your time here, remember?'

Colin nodded slowly. 'How much do you know?' he called.

'I've worked most of it out.'

'Thought you might.'

'The police came to the house. They were looking for you.'

It was true then. He was finished. He felt a deep emptiness open up inside his chest, his hollowness. His last futile hopes of escape dropped away to nothing.

234

'I didn't bring them with me, if that's what you're worried about,' Stevie went on. 'I'm on my own.'

'I'm not worried.'

'Sure you're not.'

Colin rubbed at his forehead. How am I going to get out of this, he wondered. What the hell am I going to do? 'Why did you come here?' he asked.

'I was looking for you.'

'Yes, but why?'

'So that I could talk some sense into you.'

'You want me to give myself up?'

'Yes.'

'Ha! It's a bit too bloody late for that now!'

Stevie took a step towards him and Colin jerked his hand inside his jacket pocket. 'Don't come any closer,' he shouted. 'I mean it!'

'All right.' His father settled down again, holding the top of his stick wedged in at his hip for support. He looked to be in some pain. 'Well, tell me this, then,' he called. 'What's your next move?'

'I haven't decided yet!'

'Oh, you've got two or three choices, have you?'

'Yes!'

'Bollocks! You can stay here and wait for them to come for you, or you can come with me now and we'll go into the police together. Those are your two choices.'

And there's the third, Colin thought to himself, there's always the third option and I might just do it here, in front of you.

'I can't go in!' he shouted. 'Hutchy's dead! I killed him!'

'He's not dead! They took him to hospital.'

'You're lying!'

'Why should I lie? What difference does it make to me! None! You're still in the shit, anyway. Look, you're going to have a better chance of getting out of it if you give yourself up. Or let me put it like this; if you don't give yourself up, they'll come and take you by force, and believe you me they won't give a fiddler's frig whether they get you alive or dead!'

'I'm not surrendering!'

Stevie looked away, exasperated. He stared out at the sea for a moment, then turned back to his son.

'Can I come a bit closer? Before I wreck my fucking throat as well?'

'All right . . . not too close!'

'Okay.' He limped forward until he was about ten feet from Colin. His eyes flickered over his son, taking in the mud, the torn jeans, the bruised chin. His gaze lingered on the pocket where the gun was pulling the jacket out of shape, then moved back to Colin's face.

'I can still get out,' Colin said shakily. 'I've got a plan.'

'Oh, have you? And what should that be?'

'I'll find someone . . . a hostage. They'll let me go then.'

'They'll kill you. This isn't the TV, you know. As long as they see you waving a gun, they can justify shooting you. That's all they need. And believe me, they won't think about it. And I take it that is a gun in your pocket there?'

'Might be.'

Stevie nodded slowly. 'Big lad, eh? Listen, Colin,' he said. 'You're going to prison. There's nothing you or I can do about that. You've fucked up and you'll have to pay the price. You might as well get used to that.'

'I'm not going to prison.'

'You want to end up dead, do you?'

Colin shrugged. He wished there was something he could say that was calm and witty but his thoughts were all mixed up and nothing would come out. He was at a dead end. There was no way out of this thing.

They stood for a moment, staring angrily at each other. The breeze was getting stronger, buffeting at their ears. At last Colin gestured towards the town. 'You might as well go home,' he said carelessly. 'I'm not coming in.'

'Don't be so stupid! What are you going to do?'

'I'll think of something.'

'Crap!' Stevie took a step forward and Colin tugged the pistol out, pointing it straight at his father, trying to stop the muzzle wavering.

'Stay there!' he shouted wildly. 'Stay there! Don't come any closer!'

Stevie hesitated. 'What are you going to do, shoot me?' he asked softly. 'You haven't killed anyone yet, son. You going to start now?'

They stood staring at each other for a long moment, the pistol shaking in Colin's hands. Stevie kept his eyes fixed on his son's face, never once looking at the gun.

'Go ahead,' he said. 'Shoot. You're a big man. You can do it.'

'I mean it! I'll shoot you!'

'Nah, you'll not shoot me. You haven't got that in you, have you? You're not the type. That's why you didn't shoot Kelly.'

'Shut up! I'll do it!'

237

But he knew that he wouldn't and the thought scalded him. The old man was right, he didn't have it, he didn't have that raw streak that would allow him to kill in cold blood. Hutchy had it. Hutchy would have pulled the trigger. Hutchy wouldn't have given a damn about it. He looked around at the sea and the dunes and the dark hills of Donegal away off in the distance, at the blue sky with its dusting of clouds, grown thicker now as they blew in from the sea. It's a beautiful world, he thought, closing his eyes and putting the muzzle of the pistol hard into his temple.

'Colin! No!' Stevie was shouting.

'Stay there! Don't come any closer!'

'Don't do that, Colin, Jesus fuck, please don't do that!'

There were two pressures to take up on the trigger and he remembered the man Brian telling him about them and he had taken up the first pressure but his finger had stuck there and wouldn't move. He willed it to tighten that last centimetre but it stayed in the same position, stuck fast. Total failure, he thought lucidly, can't even shoot myself, let alone anyone else.

'Colin, please!' Stevie screamed.

'There's nothing else,' he shouted back.

'Yes there is! There's everything! You're only young!'

'I've fucked it all up!'

'No! No, you haven't! You haven't killed anyone!' He stretched out his hand towards Colin as if reaching for him, the fingers splayed and shaking. 'Look, I'm sorry, all right? I'm sorry. That's what you wanted to hear. I've not been a father to you at all. I'm sorry. Now put the gun down!'

'I can't do anything else! It's all fucked up!'

238

'No! You can live! You can! Look at me! I've managed!'

'Don't start on about your fucking leg again!'

'I'm not talking about my leg!'

'What, then?'

'Years ago, in the Shankill! I killed a man! And I'm still alive, aren't I?'

It wasn't fair of the old bastard to pull something like this, Colin thought, it wasn't fair. I should do it now and to hell with him. He closed his eyes again and aimed all his willpower at the finger but still it wouldn't move. He opened his eyes again and there were tears streaming down his father's face.

'Who did you kill?' he called out.

'A wee lad.'

'You didn't know his name?'

'No.'

Jesus. That was bad.

'Why then? Why did you kill him?'

'Put the gun down and I'll tell you.'

'Tell me now or I'll do it!' Colin screamed.

'All right! All right!' Stevie wiped his mouth with the back of his hand, gathered his thoughts. 'All right. It was a club off the Shankill. They hauled this wee lad in and said he was working for the police. I knew he wasn't. They set him up on the bar in front of everybody and they handed me the gun. It was a test. They knew there was someone passing information and they thought it was me. He was eighteen. It took me seven shots to kill the poor bastard.'

Colin stared at his father, not believing what he was hearing. His father was a murderer. All this time and he hadn't known. He felt suddenly ridiculous with the gun to his head and he lowered it, holding it close in to his thigh.

'Does Mum know?' he asked. Stevie shook his head.

'Only you and me. And Mullan, he knew.'

'Mullan knew? How the fuck did Mullan know?'

'Never mind.'

'Tell me! Tell me, you old bastard! Jesus Christ, you hardly ever spoke to me before, at least tell me this now!'

'Because it was me!' Stevie spat suddenly, his voice twisted with venom. 'Because it was me! I was passing the information! I was working for the fucking Special Branch!'

It was all too much and Colin spun round, looking up into the sky, at the sea, back towards the town. Now the world was really upside down. His father was a murderer and a police informant. Terrific. He turned round again, suddenly angry.

'Why didn't you tell me?' he shouted, storming right up to his father, shouting into his face. 'Why the hell didn't you tell me! All this time! If you'd only told me that I never would have come this way!'

'I tried to tell you – '

'No! No, you tried to tell me what to do! You tried to give me orders because that was all you ever fucking did! You never once sat me down and talked to me, did you? Did you!' He prodded his father roughly in the shoulder with the pistol. 'That was why you used to cry in the toilet, wasn't it? It wasn't the fucking leg, it was your fucking conscience, and you never once told me, you never once warned me! Jesus Christ!'

Stevie rubbed at his eyes, weeping openly now. His

cheeks were shiny wet with tears. 'He was about your age, a bit younger maybe. Blond, he was. He was terrified. They gave him a beating first and his eyes were half-closed but he saw me all right, he saw me. If I hadn't shot him they would have killed me but let me tell you this, Colin, there isn't a day that goes by when I don't wish they had. I'll see his face until the day I die, right in front of me. Dear God, I'll never forget that.' His voice broke into a sob, a tear trickled down his cheek. 'You see, I killed him. I murdered him. My life is fucked up now, but yours isn't. You haven't killed anyone, you're all right!'

Colin let the pistol drop until it was hanging by his side. He felt choked and wanted to cry but tears wouldn't come. Stevie sobbed again, shielding his eyes with his hand as though embarrassed. Suddenly it was all very clear to Colin, why Mullan had called to the house so often, why he and Stevie had been so friendly. Stevie had been a police agent all along. That was why they had to move to the coast. Maybe that was the reason for the bomb and the leg, too.

'It's not the prison, Colin,' Stevie went on, choking through his tears. 'That's nothing. That passes. You'll always get out of prison. It's the faces of the men you've killed because they keep coming back and you never lose them. Never. You were lucky today. Or wise. But you haven't killed anyone. You'll only have a few years. I'm doing time for the rest of my life.'

They were both weeping openly now, shoulders shaking and tears streaming down their cheeks. Colin had never felt so confused. His world had collapsed around him. His father was a murderer. He was a murderer's son. He had been nearly a murderer himself. But Stevie had been working for the cops. But still he was a murderer. It was like a roundabout spinning madly in his head, and he couldn't think how to stop it.

The air between them seemed to twang with the desire for contact, then suddenly the old man moaned, dropping his stick in the sand as he rushed forward and threw his arms around his son. Colin smelled the faint hint of aftershave and the tobacco smell from his clothes. It was the first time his father had ever hugged him. He didn't know what to do. He moved his arms, gently, awkwardly, stretching them around his father's shaking back, still with the pistol in his right hand, pulling the old man closer to him, crying all the harder.

'It's okay, Dad,' he sobbed, 'It's okay. I'm safe now. I'm safe.'

He opened his hand and let the pistol fall and heard it thud onto the sand. He felt instantly lighter. He felt new. There was a new story beginning and he would have to go to prison but it wouldn't be for so long, really. And the world would wait. He looked past the old man's shoulders and saw the seagulls wheeling over the dunes and the sand stretching off into the distance and the white mist of spray caught by the breeze and blown back over the waves, and realised at last that the tide had turned.